THE LAMBS OF LONDON

With *The Lambs of London*, Peter Ackroyd returns to some of the obsessions of *Chatterton*, which was shortlisted for the Booker Prize. His historical fiction frequently draws inspiration from the lives and characters of real people from the past. *The Last Testament of Oscar Wilde* won the Somerset Maugham Award, while *Hawksmoor* won the Guardian Fiction Prize. His most recent historical novel, *The Clerkenwell Tales*, was a bestseller.

Peter Ackroyd is the biographer of T.S. Eliot, Dickens, Blake and Thomas More, and the author of *London: The Biography* and *Albion: The Origins of the English Imagination*. His most recent venture is *Brief Lives*, a series of short biographies, starting with *Chaucer* and *Turner*.

He has written and presented two television series for the BBC: *Dickens* (2002) and *London* (2004, accompanied by the book *Illustrated London*). He is the winner of the Whitbread Biography Award, the Royal Society of Literature's William Heinemann Award (jointly) and the James Tait Black Memorial Prize, and the holder of a CBE for services to literature.

ALSO BY PETER ACKROYD

Fiction

The Great Fire of London
The Last Testament of Oscar Wilde
Hawksmoor
Chatterton
First Light
English Music
The House of Doctor Dee
Dan Leno and the Limehouse Golem
Milton in America
The Plato Papers
The Clerkenwell Tales

Non-Fiction

London: The Biography
Dressing Up: Transvestism and Drag:
The History of an Obsession
Albion: The Origins of the English Imagination

Biography

Ezra Pound and his World
T.S. Eliot
Dickens
Blake
The Life of Thomas More

Peter Ackroyd's Brief Lives

Chaucer
Turner

Poetry

Ouch!
The Diversions of Purley and other Poems

Criticism

Notes for a New Culture
The Collection: Journalism, Reviews, Essays, Short Stories,
Lectures edited by Thomas Wright

Peter Ackroyd

THE LAMBS OF LONDON

VINTAGE

Published by Vintage 2005

2 4 6 8 10 9 7 5 3 1

Copyright © Peter Ackroyd 2004

First published in Great Britain in 2004 by
Chatto & Windus

Vintage
Random House, 20 Vauxhall Bridge Road,
London SW1V 2SA

Random House Australia (Pty) Limited
20 Alfred Street, Milsons Point, Sydney
New South Wales 2061, Australia

Random House New Zealand Limited
18 Poland Road, Glenfield,
Auckland 10, New Zealand

Random House (Pty) Limited
Endulini, 5A Jubilee Road, Parktown 2193,
South Africa

The Random House Group Limited Reg. No. 954009
www.randomhouse.co.uk/vintage

A CIP catalogue record for this book
is available from the British Library

ISBN 0 099 47209 0

Papers used by Random House are natural, recyclable
products made from wood grown in sustainable forests.
The manufacturing processes conform to the environ-
mental regulations of the country of origin

Printed and bound in Great Britain by
Bookmarque Ltd, Croydon, Surrey

This is not a biography but a work of fiction. I have invented characters, and changed the life of the Lamb family for the sake of the larger narrative.

P.A.

Chapter One

'I loathe the stench of horses.' Mary Lamb walked over to the
window, and touched very lightly the faded lace fringe of her
dress. It was a dress of the former period that she wore un-
embarrassed, as if it were of no consequence how she chose
to cover herself. 'The city is a great jakes.' There was no one
in the drawing-room with her, so she put her face upwards,
towards the sun. Her skin was marked by the scars of smallpox,
suffered by her six years before; so she held her face to the
light, and imagined it to be the pitted moon.

'I have found it, dear. It was hiding in *All's Well*.' Charles
Lamb rushed into the room with a thin green volume in his
hand.

She turned round, smiling. She did not resist her brother's
enthusiasm; it cleared her head of the moon. 'And is it?'

'Is it what, dear?'

'All's well that ends well?'

'I very much hope so.' The top buttons of his linen shirt were undone, and his stock only loosely knotted. 'May I read it to you?' He dropped into an armchair, and swiftly crossed his legs. It was a rapid and economical movement, to which his sister had become accustomed. He held out the volume at arm's length, and recited a passage. ' "They say miracles are past; and we have our philosophical persons to make things supernatural and causeless seem modern and familiar. Hence is it that we make trifles of terrors, ensconcing ourselves into seeming knowledge when we should submit ourselves to an unknown fear." Lafew to Parolles. That is exactly the thought of Hobbes.'

Mary generally read what her brother read, but she did so more slowly. She was more thoroughly absorbed; she would sit by the window, where the light had touched her a few moments before, and contemplate the sensations that her reading had aroused in her. She felt then, as she had told her brother, part of the world's spirit. She read so that she might keep up these conversations with Charles which had become the great solace of her life. They talked on those evenings when he returned, sober, from the East India House. They confided in each other, seeing the same soul shining in each other's face.

'What was that phrase, "seeming knowledge"? You enunciate so well, Charles. I would be glad to have your gift.' She admired her brother precisely to the extent that she did not admire herself.

'Words, words, words.'

'But would that apply to the people whom we know?' she asked him.

'Would what, dear?'

'Seeming knowledge and unknown fear?'

'Elaborate.'

'I seem to know Pa, but should I submit to an unknown fear concerning him?'

Their parents, on this Sunday morning, were returning from the Dissenters' chapel on the corner of Lincoln's Inn Lane and Spanish Street. They were only a hundred yards from the house, and Mary watched as her mother and father crossed slowly from lane to lane. Mr Lamb was in the first stages of senile decay, but Mrs Lamb held him upright with her powerful right arm.

'And then there is Selwyn Onions,' Mary added. He was one of Charles's clerkly colleagues in Leadenhall Street. 'I seem to know his pranks and jokes, but should I submit to an unknown fear concerning his malevolent spirit?'

'Onions? He is a good enough fellow.'

'I dare say.'

'You look too deep, dear.'

It was a day in late autumn, and the brickwork of the houses opposite was stained red with the declining sun. The street itself was littered with orange peel, scraps of newspaper and fallen leaves. An old woman, draped in a voluminous shawl, was clutching the pump on the corner.

'What is "too deep?"' She was surprised by her brother's flippancy. It was insensitive, and she relied upon his sensitivity to give meaning to her life.

'There are some subjects, Mary, which have no depth. Onions is one of them.' He was annoyed by his disloyalty towards his friend, and quickly changed the subject. 'Why is Sunday so horrid? It is my day of rest, but it is so dry and desolate. It presses the life out of me. There is nowhere to think.' He jumped up from the chair, and stood next to his sister in the bay of the window. 'It only comes alive by twilight. But by then it is too late. Now I will go to my room and study Sterne.'

She was accustomed to this. 'Being left by Charles' was, as she put it to herself, a 'compound verb' signifying a coherent and complete sensation of loss, disappointment and anticipation. She did not feel abandoned, precisely. She was hardly ever alone in the house. And here they were. She heard her mother's key in the lock, and instinctively she held herself more upright; it was as if she were warding off danger. Mr Lamb was wiping his boots on the straw mat by the door while Mrs Lamb was asking their maid-servant, Tizzy, to clear up the leaves. Mary knew that Charles would be sinking deeper into his chair, shutting out the noises of the house with Sterne. She turned back to the window, as her parents entered the room, and prepared herself to become a daughter again.

'Sit with your poor father, Mary, while I prepare an egg-nog. He may have caught cold.' He shook his head and laughed. 'What are you saying, Mr Lamb?' He looked down at her feet. 'You are quite right. I still have on my pattens. You miss nothing, I am sure.'

'Take them off,' he said. And then he laughed again.

Mary Lamb had watched her father's slow decline with interest. He had been a man of business, quick and efficient in all the dealings of the world. He had marshalled his affairs as if he were engaged in warfare with some invisible enemy and, when he returned each evening to the house in Laystall Street, he had an air of triumph. Then, one evening, he came home wide-eyed with terror. 'I don't know where I have been,' was all he said. Quietly he began to slip away. He had been Mary's father, then he became her friend and, finally, her child.

Charles Lamb seemed to pay no attention to his father's condition; he avoided him, whenever possible, and made no comment on his increasing incapacity. Whenever Mary raised the subject of 'Pa', he listened to her patiently but offered no comment. He could not speak of it.

Mr Lamb was rubbing his hands eagerly, in anticipation of the egg-nog.

When her mother had left the room, Mary sat down beside him on the faded green divan. 'Did you sing at the service, Pa?'

'The minister was mistaken.'

'On what matter?'

'There are no rabbits in Worcestershire.'

'Are there not?'

'No, nor muffins neither.'

Mrs Lamb professed to believe that there was some wisdom in her husband's ramblings, but Mary knew that there was none. Yet he interested her more now than he had ever done; she was intrigued by the strange and random phrases that issued from him. It was as if language was talking to itself.

'Are you cold, Pa?'

'Just an error in the accounts.'

'Do you suppose?'

'A red letter day.'

Mrs Lamb returned with the egg-nog in a bowl. 'Mary dear,

you are keeping your father from the fire.' She was perpetually watchful, as if something in the world was forever trying to elude her. 'Where is your brother?'

'Reading.'

'That is a surprise. Drink it carefully, Mr Lamb. Mary, help your father.'

Mary did not like her mother very much. She was a prying and inquisitive woman, or so Mary thought; her mother's watchfulness seemed to her to be a form of hostility. It never occurred to Mary that it was a form of fear.

'Don't slurp, Mr Lamb. Your linen will be soiled.'

Mary gently took the bowl from him, and began to feed him with the porcelain spoon. She spent her life performing such tasks. Tizzy was too frail to deal with all the household cleaning and cooking, so Mary took on the most onerous duties. They could have afforded a young servant, at no more than ten shillings per week, but Mrs Lamb objected in principle to the introduction of another person who might shatter the carefully preserved composition, and the calm, of the Lamb family.

Mary accepted her role willingly enough. Charles went to the office, and she 'saw to' the house. That was how it would always be. After her sickness, in any case, she had become more subdued. The scars upon her face had made her an object of pity or distaste – or so she thought – and she had no wish to show herself.

She could hear Charles pacing the floor, in the room above. She had become accustomed to his footsteps and knew that he was preparing to write; he was placing his thoughts in order before he began. He was treading upon a narrow strip of carpet at the foot of his bed, and after three or four more 'turns' he would sit at his desk and begin. He had been introduced to the editor of *Westminster Words*, Matthew Law, who had been charmed by the young man's discourse on the acting style at the Old Drury Lane; he had commissioned from him an essay on the subject, and Charles had completed it only three days later. He had ended with a flourish, on the acting of Munden, when he had said that 'A tub of butter, contemplated by him, amounts to a Platonic idea. He understands a leg of mutton in its quiddity. He stands wondering, amid the common-place materials of life, like primeval man with the sun and stars about him.' This was considered to be a 'mighty flare', according to Matthew Law, and since then Charles had become a regular contributor to the weekly paper. At this moment he was writing an article in praise of chimney sweeps. He had been reading Sterne to discover whether his favourite novelist had ever entertained the topic.

Charles continued to earn his living as a clerk at the East India House, as his mother had insisted, but he wished to consider himself to be a writer. Ever since his school-days as a poor scholar at Christ's Hospital, all his hopes and ambitions had been directed towards literature. He would read his poems to Mary; and she would listen very carefully, almost solemnly. It was as if she had written them herself. He had written a drama in which he had played Darnley and she had played Mary Queen of Scots; she had been deeply excited by her role, and still remembered some of the lines she had spoken.

'Call your brother to dinner, Mary.'

'He is busy with his essay, Ma.'

'His essay will not be affected by pork chops, I dare say.'

Mr Lamb made a remark about red hair, which neither woman noticed.

Mary had gone to the door, but Charles was already half-way down the stairs.

'There is pork in the air, dear. The strong man may batten on him, and the weakling refuseth not his mild juices.'

'Francis Bacon?'

'No. Charles Lamb. A subtler dish. *Buon giorno*, Ma.'

Mrs Lamb was guiding her husband towards the small dining-room at the rear of the house; it overlooked a narrow strip of garden, at the bottom of which were a cast-iron pagoda and the remains of a bonfire of leaves. On the previous morning she and Mary had gathered up the leaves in armfuls, from the clipped grass and the slate path, before setting light to them; Mary had breathed in the scent as the sweet smoke rose towards the clouded London sky. It was as if she were performing a sacrifice – but to what strange god? Could it be the god of childhood?

Tizzy was putting a dish of sauce upon the table; she had a slight palsy, and spilled some upon the waxen polished surface. Charles licked his finger and scooped it up. 'A few breadcrumbs, mixed with liver and a dash of mild sage. It is bliss.'

'Nonsense, Charles.' Mrs Lamb was a member of the Holborn Fundamental Communion, and had firm ideas on the subject of bliss. Her somewhat dour piety, however, had no obvious effect upon her appetite. She intoned the grace, in which her children joined, and then served the chops.

'Why should the act of eating need a blessing?' Charles had once asked his sister. 'As distinct from silent gratitude? Why not a grace before setting out on a moonlight ramble? A grace before Spenser? A grace before a friendly meeting?' Ever since childhood Mary had disliked the ceremony of the family meal. The handling of the plates, the serving of the food, the chinking of the cutlery, induced in her a kind of weariness. On these occasions, only Charles could lift her spirits. 'I wonder,' he said now, 'who was the greatest fool who ever lived. Will Somers? Justice Shallow?'

'Really, Charles. You forget yourself.' Mrs Lamb was looking in the general direction of her husband, without seeming to single him out.

Mary laughed, and in the sudden movement a piece of potato lodged in her throat. She got up quickly, gasping for air; her mother rose from the table, but she waved her violently away. She did not want to be touched by her. She coughed the potato into her hand, and sighed.

'Who will buy my sweet oranges?' asked her father.

Mrs Lamb resumed her seat and continued eating her meal. 'You came home very late, Charles.'

'I was dining with friends, Ma.'

'Is that what you call it?'

Charles had come back to Laystall Street very drunk. Mary waited up for him, as always, and as soon as she heard him trying vainly to find the lock she opened the door and held him as he staggered forward. He drank too much on two or three evenings each week; he was 'sozzled', as he would put it apologetically the next day, but Mary never rebuked him. She believed that she understood the reasons for his drunkenness, and even sympathised with them. Had she the courage or the opportunity, she would be drunk every day of her life.

To be buried alive – was that not motive enough to drink? Charles was in any case a writer, and writers were well known for their indulgence. What of Sterne or Smollett? Not that her brother was ever loud or belligerent; he was as mild and as amiable as ever, except that he could not stand or speak with any degree of precision. '*It is the cause, it is the cause,*' he had said to Mary the previous night. 'Lead on.'

He had been drinking sweet wine and Burton ale at the Salutation and Cat in Hand Court, close by Lincoln's Inn Fields, with two colleagues from the East India House, Tom Coates and Benjamin Milton. They were both very short, dapper, and dark-haired; they spoke quickly and laughed immoderately at each other's remarks. Charles was a little younger than Coates, and a little older than Milton, and so he felt himself to be – as he put it to them – 'the neutral medium through which galvanic forces can be conducted'. Coates spoke of Spinoza and of Schiller, of biblical inspiration and the romantic imagination; Milton spoke of geology and the ages of the earth, of fossils and dead seas. As he became drunker, Lamb imagined himself to be in the infancy of the world. What might be achieved, in a society that had such great intellects within it?

'Did I wake you last night, Ma?'

'I was already awake. Mr Lamb was restless.' Her husband had a habit of trying to urinate out of the bedroom window on to the street beneath, a habit to which Mrs Lamb was strenuously opposed.

'You were very quiet, Charles.' Mary was now calm after her fit of coughing. 'You went straight to your bed.'

'I live forever in your good report, Mary. The heavens shine down on such a sister.'

'I distinctly heard a noise from your room.' Mrs Lamb was not impressed by their show of affection. 'There was a crash.'

In fact Mary had helped her brother to mount the stairs, and had guided him towards his bedroom. She held his arm gently, and savoured the vinous scent of his breath mixed with the faintest odour of sweat on his neck and forehead. She enjoyed the sensation of his physical closeness, which in the past she had lost. He had been a boarder at Christ's Hospital, and his departure at the beginning of each term provoked in her the strangest mixture of anger and loneliness. He was going to a world of companionship and learning, while she was left in the company of her mother and of Tizzy. This was the period when, her household tasks complete, she began to study. Her bedroom had been set up in a little back room on the attic floor. Here she kept the school-books which Charles had lent her – among them a Latin grammar, a Greek lexicon, Voltaire's *Philosophical Dictionary* and a copy of *Don Quixote*. She tried to keep pace with her brother but often found, on his return, that she had over-reached him. She had begun to read and to translate the fourth book of the *Aeneid*, concerning the love between Dido and Aeneas, before he had even mastered the speeches of Cicero. She had said to him, '*At regina gravi iamdudum saucia cura*'; but he had burst out laughing. 'Whatever do you mean, dear?'

'It is Virgil, Charles. Dido is sorrowful.'

He laughed again, and ruffled her hair. She tried to smile but then lowered her head; she felt vain and foolish.

But there were other occasions when they would study together in the evenings, both of them poring over one book, their eyes alight as they pursued the same sentence. They would talk of Roderick Random and of Peregrine Pickle as if they were real people, and invent new scenes or adventures for Lemuel Gulliver and Robinson Crusoe. They would imagine themselves to be on Crusoe's island, hiding in the foliage from the marauding cannibals. And then they would return to the intricacies of Greek syntax. He told her that she had become 'a Grecian'.

'A crash, Ma?' He asked the question with a sense of injured innocence. He really did not know what she meant.

He had toppled on to his bed, and had immediately fallen into a profound sleep; it was as if he had finally escaped.

Mary untied his boots, and began to pull one off his right foot; but she slipped and fell backwards against his desk, knocking off a candlestick and a small brass bowl in which he kept spent lucifer matches. This was the crash that Mrs Lamb, awake and alert across the landing, had heard. It had not woken Charles. In the silence which followed Mary gently put back the candlestick and the bowl; she removed his boots very slowly, and then lay down beside him. She put her arms around him and placed her head upon his chest, so softly that it rose and fell with his breathing. A few minutes later she crept up the stairs to her own little room.

After the meal was over it was customary, on Sunday, for Charles to read from the Bible to his parents and sister. He did not object to this in the least. He admired the artifice of the King James version. Its periodic balance, its cadence and its euphony had come upon him in childhood like the wind. '*I saw a dream which made me afraid, and the thoughts upon my bed and the visions of my head troubled me.*' They had gathered in the drawing-room, where Mary had stood in the sunlight, and Charles was behind a small leaved table with the volume in his hand. 'This, Pa, is the story of Nebuchadnezzar.'

'Is it indeed? How did he know when to cry?'

'When God chided him, Mr Lamb.' Mrs Lamb was very emphatic. 'All flesh is grass.'

Instinctively Mary put her hand up to her face, as Charles continued his reading from Daniel. '*Therefore made I a decree to bring in all the wise men of Babylon before me, that they might make known unto me the interpretation of the dream.*'

Chapter Two

On the following morning Charles Lamb left the house in Holborn on his way to the East India House in Leadenhall Street. When he came out of Holborn Passage he joined the vast throng of pedestrians moving towards the City on this bright autumn morning. Yet he had seen something – he was sure of it – and he turned back. He had risen early, and he had at least one hour before he needed to sit before his high desk in the Dividend Office. Holborn Passage itself was little more than an alley, one of those dark threads woven into the city's fabric which accumulate soot and dust over the centuries. There was a pipe shop here as well as a mantua-maker, a carpenter's workshop and a bookshop. All of them wore with resignation the faded patina of age and abandonment. The gowns were discoloured, the pipes on display would never be smoked, and the workshop seemed untenanted. Yes. This was what he had seen. In the window of the bookshop was displayed a document, written in a sixteenth-century Secretary hand.

Charles loved all the tokens of antiquity. He had stood on the site of the old Aldgate pump, and imagined water being drawn from the wooden pipe five hundred years before; he had paced the line of the Roman wall, and noticed how the streets naturally conformed to it; he had lingered over the sundials in the Inner Temple, and traced their mottoes with his finger. 'The future is as nothing, being everything,' he had once told Tom Coates in a moment of drunken inspiration. 'The past is everything, being nothing.'

This Elizabethan document seemed to be a will; he was not a palaeographer, but he could make out the phrase 'I bequethe'. A young man, standing in the dim interior of the shop, was staring at him from the other side of the window. With his pale face, and violently red hair, he seemed to Charles to be some kind of apparition. Then he smiled and opened the door. 'Mr Lamb?'

'The very same. How do you know my name?'

'You have been pointed out to me in the Salutation and Cat. I sit there sometimes at the back table. You would not have noticed me in the least. Come in, please.'

As soon as he entered the shop Charles could smell the moth-scented coverings of the old folios and quartos; it was the dust of learning he inhaled, delicious in its specialty. There was a wooden counter around two sides of the room, upon which were laid out manuscripts, unbound sheets and parchment rolls. On the shelves he could see the collected works of Drayton, Drummond of Hawthornden and Cowley. 'In some respects,' the young man said, noticing his glance, 'the better a book is, the less it demands from the binding. To be strong-backed and neat bound is the desideratum of a volume.'

'Magnificence comes after?'

'If it comes at all. My name is Ireland, Mr Lamb. William Henry Ireland.' They shook hands. 'I would not dress a set of magazines, for instance, in full suit. There is no point in a Shakespeare in gorgeous apparel.'

Charles was surprised by this young man's expertness. 'You are quite right. The true lover of reading, Mr Ireland, wishes for sullied leaves and worn-out appearance.'

'I know the difference, Mr Lamb. I know the pages turned with delight, not with duty.'

'You do?' Here was a rare young man indeed.

William Ireland was, as Charles surmised, a youth of about seventeen years; in his cravat, shirt and bright yellow waist-coat he seemed a curiously old-fashioned figure. He ought to have been wearing a powdered wig. Yet his intensity was such that Charles was drawn to him. 'I prefer the common editions of Shakespeare,' Ireland was saying, 'without notes and without platcs. Your Rowe or your Tonson delights me. On the contrary, I cannot read Beaumont and Fletcher but in folio. The octavo editions are painful to look at, don't you think? I have no sympathy with them. I abhor them.' He had pale green eyes, which widened with the inflections of his voice; when he spoke he clasped his hands together, as if he were engaged in a violent struggle with himself. 'Do you care for Drayton, Mr Lamb?'

'Extremely.'

'Then this will interest you.' He took down from its shelf a quarto volume, neatly bound in calf. 'This is Greene's *Pandosto*. But note the inscription.' He opened the book, and handed it to Charles. On the frontispiece, traced in now faded ink, were the words '*Given to me, Mich. Drayton, by Will Sh.*'.

Charles knew well enough that *Pandosto* had been the source for *A Winter's Tale*. And here was the book itself, the book that Shakespeare had held in his hands – just as he was holding it now. The sheer reciprocity of the gesture almost made him swoon.

William Ireland was looking at him intently, willing him to speak.

'It is a most remarkable thing.' Charles closed the book and carefully put it down upon the counter. 'How did you acquire it?'

'From a gentleman's library. He died last year. Father and I travelled down to Wiltshire. There were treasures there, Mr Lamb. Treasures.' He placed the book upon the shelf, and spoke with his back turned. 'Father owns the shop.'

He had travelled with his father on the Salisbury coach, three weeks ago. They were late passengers, having booked their tickets only two days before, and were asked to sit in the open seats behind the driver and his three horses. 'No, no,' Samuel Ireland had said. 'I must travel within. This September air is piercing.'

'How is it possible, sir?' The driver, like all who encountered the elder Ireland, was subdued by his over-bearing manner.

'I will tell you how it is possible. By doing it.' Mr Ireland clambered into the coach, and turned to his son. 'You may go on top, William. It will revive you.' He took off his beaver hat, offered elaborate courtesies to the only lady in the vehicle, and then slowly inserted himself between two male passengers like a cork being put back in a bottle. 'I beg your pardon, sir,' he said to each of them in turn. 'Just one inch more, if you please. Profound apologies.'

William Ireland had already climbed the ladder, and crouched upon a seat as the stage rattled down Cornhill and Cheapside towards St Paul's. He looked up as the horses passed the cathedral. He could not imagine on what principles it had been constructed, or the serenity in the soul of the architect who had conceived it. The great dome was, for him, an alien thing.

He was by now quite accustomed to his father's selfishness – except that he never would have used that word. He was peremptory, magisterial, eloquent. But he was a bookseller. He was only a tradesman. And William knew that he suffered exquisitely for that. His father's regard for himself was his only way of continuing and enduring life.

There was a lock of horses and carriages on Ludgate Hill, and the stage slowly came to a halt. William looked back at the dome. He would never achieve anything that might rival this. He was the thing he was. Nothing more. In this momentary pause, above the sounds of London, he could hear his father's voice in the carriage beneath. He was discoursing on the virtues of truffles.

The stage stopped at an inn in Bagshot, so that the outside passengers might be warmed. William sat by the small coal fire in the parlour, clutching a cup of hot porter; he was sitting with Beryl who, as he had already learnt, was a lady's maid who had lost her position and was returning to her family in the country. 'It's not so much the leaving,' she said, 'as the manner of the leaving.' She was utterly defiant. 'Here's two guineas, and out the door.' William did not wish to enquire too closely into the reasons for her dismissal but, judging by her demeanour, he suspected some back-stairs lust. 'I took her shawl, anyway. She'll never miss it. Where did you come by that kerchief?'

'My father's.'

'Is he the one who does all the talking?' They had been the only passengers sitting on top of the stage, and had formed an unspoken alliance against those more comfortably placed.

'I'm afraid so.' Samuel Ireland was even then regaling his travelling companions with the true components of the drink known as 'Stingo'. He might have been discussing the merits of Shakespeare. Anything he related became, of necessity, important. 'How did you know that was my father?'

'He has your features. Except that yours are nicer. What's your name?'

'William.'

'Bill? Or Will? Or would it be Willy?'

'William, actually.'

'William the Conqueror.' She looked down at the buttons on his trousers, for only a moment; but it was enough to stir him. He felt tense and excited, as if he were about to suffer some immense shock. He clutched his cup to stop his hands from shaking. 'Is it standing up, William?'

'Yes. It is.'

'Is it big?'

'I don't know. I have no ' He had never before been approached in this way. Even in the streets the prostitutes turned away from him as a boy, and a poor boy at that; he had pleasured himself, as he put it, but he had never done this.

The other passengers were enjoying all the smells and

sensations of the inn, as if they were characters in a stage play entitled *The Parlour*. They were good-humoured, tolerant, disposed to laugh. Samuel Ireland, one arm raised in the air, was now modestly alluding to his friendship with Richard Brinsley Sheridan. William's heart was beating faster. The coachman, having received two shillings from the landlord of the inn, came to the door of the parlour and asked them back to the coach. William rushed out, before any of the others could see him, and ascended the ladder to the roof of the stage. He saw Beryl walking slowly across the yard, and he put his hands between his legs. She climbed on to the roof and, with a smile, sat in the seat furthest from him. The coachman jumped into his box, raised his whip, and cried out to the horses. As they left the inn-yard Beryl came over to William, and put her hand upon his fly. Then she began to massage his inner thighs. The carriage jerked up and down the uneven surface of Bagshot High Street. It was essentially a country lane, paved at the expense of the landlord himself. No one from the road could see her hand – the driver looked ahead – and she paddled his cock with increasing vigour. When they came out into the open fields, travelling past small streams and copses of trees, fields and hedgerows, she hitched up her skirt and settled herself upon the roof of the carriage. Some wild geese flew overhead. He unbuttoned his trousers and lay down upon her. He could feel the cold wind rushing upon his face, and he sighed with delight. He moved gently within her. Then he grew stronger and more vigorous; as the coachman called out 'Hi!', he came within her. They were riding through the hamlet of Blackwater, and so both of them lay very still in order to escape notice. He fumbled with his trousers, and secured the buttons, before getting to his feet.

She still lay upon the roof, and looked up at the passing sky.

William's first and greatest sensation was that of relief. He had done the unknown thing, and had not wavered. Beryl pulled up her under-drawers before clambering into her seat. Then, with a smile, she held out her hand. It was an unmistakable gesture.

'I only have a few sixpences,' he said.

'They'll do.'

He felt in the pocket of his trousers, and gave her the coins. Together they gazed at the passing landscape, as they drove on to Stonehenge and Salisbury.

'What kind of treasures?' Charles was asking him as they stood in the bookshop together.

'An original *De Sphaera* from the printing shop of Manutius. A second edition of Erasmus, printed in France.'

These were not books that excited Charles's imagination. He was more at ease among the old English authors. So he took down Greene's *Pandosto* from the shelf where William had placed it. 'Is this altogether too expensive?'

'Three guineas.' Charles noticed that he spoke in a harsh, impetuous manner; as if he were daring others to challenge him.

'Three guineas will buy a lot of books.'

'Not ones with such an owner.'

It was a week's wage. Yet to own a book that had once been owned by Shakespeare – it was worth more than a week of his life. 'I can leave you a guinea, and pay the rest when I come for the book.'

'No need to trouble yourself, Mr Lamb. I am happy to bring

it to you.' William Ireland went behind the counter, and brought out a leather-bound ledger. He took an ink-pot and quill from the pocket of his coat, much to Charles's astonishment, and proceeded to write out the receipt. Charles noticed that he had a neat Chancery hand, quite unlike the Secretary hand he himself used for the Company's accounts, and he complimented him upon it. 'I learnt it from my father, Mr Lamb. I take a good deal of pleasure in it. I use a Court hand for certain transactions. And a Text hand for the general business of life.'

'You will need an address.'

'I know the house.' He did not look up.

Two nights before, William Ireland had led Charles home from the Salutation and Cat. Charles had been drinking there alone. He had been sitting at an old ebony table in a corner; on the wall behind him was an embroidered handkerchief in a glass case. Its motto had faded but the phrase 'well bake a pie' could still be traced.

Charles was staring at nothing in particular. He was scratching his chin with his forefinger. He had often entertained the possibility of catching his elusive thoughts and placing them in sequence – so many impressions and associations, so many rambles around the mind – but he had not yet achieved it. He swallowed down another glass of curaçao, its sweetness now beginning to curdle in his stomach. But he did not wish to return to Laystall Street. He did not like the smell of the house at night, which reminded him of kitchen slops. He had no desire to see his parents, who seemed to close down the possibilities of life. And as for Mary, well, certainly he enjoyed her company. But there were times when her attention to him, intense and sensitive, repelled him. He needed her society to expand, to flourish, to become himself; she applauded him because she understood him. But when she made too large a claim upon him – when for example she questioned him too insistently about his friendships – he withdrew from her and became quiet. Then she in turn felt humiliated and rejected. So there were evenings when he drank alone.

He considered it foolish to suppose that alcohol was a source of inspiration. He knew that it constrained his imagination, confining it to the layers of drunken perception. When he was drunk, he was oblivious to detail or perspective. Yet he welcomed, and actively sought, this state. It relieved him from fear and responsibility. But what did he fear? He feared his own failure. He feared his future. One of his school companions, Tobias Smith, had left Christ's Hospital without a post or vocation. He had lived with his mother for a while in Smithfield and, in the tavern or playhouse, seemed to be as gay and vivacious as ever. Yet he had declined. His clothes had become threadbare. When his mother died, he was thrown out of the shared lodgings. He seemed to disappear. But then, three weeks ago, Charles had seen him begging on the corner of Coleman Street. He passed him without showing any sign of recognition. He had been afraid. So now he drank the curaçao.

He savoured the sensations of slipping into drunkenness. He could not recall his state of infancy, but he guessed that it must have been something like this – this blissful reception of circumstance, this happy acceptance of everything in the world. He went up to the counter and ordered another glass. He sensed his need to talk even as he asked the landlord a question about that evening's customers. He wanted to divulge news about himself; he wanted to laugh out loud at someone else's wit.

'This one will be the last, Mr Lamb.'

'Of course. Yes.'

And then he found himself sprawled upon his bed, fully dressed. He could recall nothing from the night before. He had images of giant shadows in turmoil, of an outstretched arm, of a whispered word. He had no recollection of William Ireland, who had been seated by the door of the Salutation and Cat; Ireland had in fact been partially obscured by a wooden pillar around which various advertisements – for a harlequinade, for an exhibition of acrobatics – had been pasted.

Charles had returned to his seat from the counter; he had thrown back his head and drained the last glass of curaçao. He had risen unsteadily to his feet, and then moved wide-eyed in the general direction of the door. He had said, out loud, *'You that way, we this way.'*

William Ireland got up from his chair and, with great gentleness, helped Charles into the street. The drunken man would become an immediate target of pick-pockets, or worse, and so he guided him away from Lincoln's Inn Fields.

'Where do you lodge, sir?'

Charles laughed at the question. 'I lodge in eternity.'

'That may be difficult to find.' Yet Charles walked along King Street and Little Queen Street, towards Laystall Street, instinctively turning towards home. 'You quoted from Shakespeare just then. *You that way, we this way. Love's Labour's Lost.*'

'Did I? This way now.'

A member of the local watch passed and shone a lantern in William's face. 'My friend is tired,' William said. 'I am accompanying him home.' Calling Charles his friend allowed a degree of intimacy. He linked arms with him and steadied him as they turned into Laystall Street.

William had heard and seen him before in the Salutation and Cat. Charles often sat there with his companions. They talked loudly about the latest plays and publications; they argued over philosophy, or the merits of certain actresses. Ireland himself was always alone and, sitting in his customary place by the door, listened eagerly. He could make out bursts or gusts of conversation, and had in particular been impressed by an oration given by Charles on the virtues of Dryden as opposed to Pope. William had discovered, too, that Charles wrote for the periodicals; he had overheard his discussion of a proposed essay on the topic of poor relations. 'They are always smiling and they are always embarrassed,' he was saying to Tom Coates and Benjamin Milton. 'And they are a puzzle to the servants, who are fearful of being either too obsequious or too uncivil.'

'But you have no servants.'

'Is Tizzy nothing? A toast to Tizzy! A toast to no one!'

William had himself submitted an essay to the *Pall Mall Review*, on Renaissance bindings, but it had been rejected on the grounds that it was 'too singular a subject for a general readership'. He had not been surprised by this response. His ambition was matched only by his self-distrust; he aspired to success but expected failure. So he listened to Charles with envy and admiration; he envied those around him, too, who seemed thoroughly at home in the world of literature and journalism. If he could become acquainted with Mr Lamb, then he might enter this charmed fellowship.

He hoped, too, that he might follow Charles Lamb's own path. To write – to be published – these were his ambitions. His essay for the *Pall Mall Review* had been his only attempt at publication. But he had also written certain odes and sonnets. He thought highly of his 'Ode on Liberty. On the Occasion of Napoleon's Return to France from Egypt' but he knew that, in the present circumstances, it could not be printed in the English journals. In other odes he had railed against England's 'muddy darkness' and 'dreary bounds'. In his sonnets he had pursued a vein of more private sentiment, and in one sequence had charted the history of a 'man of feeling' who was ignored or ridiculed by 'the brute mass of humankind'. He had not shown these works to anyone but had kept them locked in his writing-case, from which he occasionally took them out and read them over. He considered them to be the centre of his true life, but there was no one on earth with whom he could share them. As he had once written:

> Still and inert my mental powers lie
> Without the quick'ning spark of Sympathy.

He believed that he might obtain that from Charles Lamb and his friends. But he could never have crossed the room. There was a gulf too deep; it was the gulf of self-abnegation.

William guided Charles down the narrow street, avoiding the pump and making sure that he did not fall against the damp and sooty brick wall of the bakery on the corner. It was called 'Stride. Our Baker'. Every weekday morning – what he called a 'school morning' – Charles would pick up a penny loaf and eat it on his way to Leadenhall Street. Now he passed it without recognition. Only by instinct did he climb the steps from the cobbled pavement to his own door. William stood behind him as he fumbled for his keys, but then the door was opened by a young woman. William walked quickly down Laystall Street, for some reason fearful of being seen by her.

But Mary Lamb had not noticed him at all, intent only on helping her brother once more across the threshold of their little house.

'How do you know it?'

'How do I know your address, Mr Lamb? I escorted you home the other evening. There is no reason why you should remember.' He managed to suggest that it was his own insignificance, rather than Charles's drunkenness, that had caused this lapse of memory.

'From the Salutation?'

William nodded.

Charles had grace enough to blush; but his voice was composed. He had a strange relationship with his drunken self; he considered him to be an unhappy and unfortunate acquaintance to whom he had become accustomed. He would neither defend him nor apologise for him. He would simply recognise his existence. 'Well, I am obliged to you. Could you call this evening?'

They shook hands. Charles stepped out of the bookshop, looking left and right before he walked out of the dark passage into High Holborn. He joined the throng of carriages and pedestrians, all moving eastward into the City. It was for him a motley parade, part funeral procession and part pantomime, evincing to him the fullness and variety of life in all its aspects – before the City swallowed it up. The sound of footsteps on the cobbles mingled with the rumble of the carriage wheels and the echo of horse hooves to make what Charles considered to be a uniquely city sound. It was the music of movement itself. There were caps and bonnets and hats bobbing in the distance; there were purple frock-coats and green jackets, striped top-coats and check surtouts, umbrellas and great woollen parti-coloured shawls, all around him. Charles himself always dressed in black and, being surprisingly angular, he resembled a young and awkward clergyman. A flying pie man knew him by sight, and sold him a veal pastie.

He was part of the crowd. There were times when this brought him comfort, when he considered himself to be part of the texture of life. There were occasions when it merely reinforced his sense of failure. More often than not, however, it spurred his ambition. He envisaged the days when, from his comfortable library or writing-room, he would be able to hear the crowd passing by.

He knew the road so well that he scarcely noticed it; he was borne along past Snow Hill and Newgate, along Cheapside, and up Cornhill; until he found himself in Leadenhall Street. It was as if he had been fired from a cannon into the pillared portico of the East India House. It was an old mansion house, from the days of Queen Anne, built of brick and stone and powerfully reinforced by a great cupola that cast a shadow on an already dark and dusty Leadenhall Street. Charles squeezed the arm of the door-keeper as he passed him, and whispered, 'Vermiculated rustication.' They had been debating, the previous Saturday, the name of the worm-like ornamentation on the base of the building where it met the street. The door-keeper put a hand to his forehead, and pretended to topple back in astonishment.

Charles passed into the entrance hall, the quick patter of his shoes sending little flickers of noise among the marble pillars, and he mounted the great ornamental staircase two steps at a time.

There were six clerks in the Dividend Office where Charles worked. Their desks were set up in the pattern of an inverted 'V' – or, as Charles put it, 'like a flight of geese' – with the head clerk at the front. There was a long low table running down the middle of this formation, supporting various leather-bound volumes of accounts and registers. Each clerk sat on a high-backed chair behind his desk, with pen and ink and blotter neatly arranged. Benjamin Milton sat in front of Charles, Tom Coates behind.

Benjamin turned when he heard the familiar scrape of the chair. 'Good morning to you, Charlie. It was never merry in England till you were born.'

'I know. I am witty in myself, and the cause of wit in others.'

Benjamin was a short slim youth, dark-haired and hand-some. Charles called him 'the pocket-sized Garrick' after the late actor-manager. Like Garrick, Benjamin seemed to be perpetually cheerful.

Tom Coates arrived, crooning the latest ballad melody. He was always in love, and always in debt. He would weep copi-ously at a romance in the penny-gaffs and then, at the next moment, begin to laugh at his own sentimentality. 'I love my mother,' he said. 'She has knitted me these gloves.' Charles did not turn round to admire them. The head clerk, Solomon Jarvis, had risen from his seat and was about to distribute the single-column and double-column ledgers. Jarvis was a grave man, an employee for forty years who still felt it an honour to be an East India clerk. Whatever ambition or aspiration he had once harboured, it had come to nothing. Yet he was not a disappointed man – serious, solemn, but not disappointed. He was one of the last clerks to wear his hair powdered and frizzed out in the old manner; it was not clear whether he preferred the fashion of the previous reign out of stubborn antiquarianism or out of some hallowed remembrance of his appearance as a 'beau' or 'macaroni'. In any case he was, as Benjamin used to say, 'a living obelisk'. He was also addicted to snuff, and would take out vast quantities from the pockets of his ancient rust-coloured waistcoat. Charles claimed in fact that his hair was covered in snuff rather than powder, but the theory was never put to the test.

'Gentlemen,' Jarvis was saying, 'a dividend day will soon be upon us. Shall we calculate? Shall we work on the warrants?'

They wrote out their numbers beneath a fresco by Sir James Thornhill, showing Industry and Prosperity being greeted on the shore of the Bay of Calcutta by three Indian princes who held in their hands the various fruits of that region. In exchange Industry offered a hoe while Prosperity showed them a pair of golden scales. Charles was more interested in the painted sea and landscape. He would put his hands behind his head and gaze at the ceiling, letting his eyes wander among the distant blues and greens. He imagined the thud of the ocean on foreign shores, and the whisper of a warm breeze among the flowing trees, until he was roused by the scratching of the pens all around him.

He was writing down three round 'O's, at the end of a calculation, when the bell sounded at the conclusion of that day's labour. Tom Coates was already by his chair. 'What sayest thou, Charlie? Just the one?' They were joined by Benjamin Milton, who put his hand to his lips and imitated the call of a bugle.

'Well,' Charles replied. 'Just the one.'

The three young men clattered out of the building into Leadenhall Street. They walked quickly over the stones, their hands in their pockets, their black frock-coats fluttering out behind them; they turned into Billiter Street, patting the flanks of the horses as they dodged between them, and strode into the welcome warmth of the Billiter Inn where the low murmur of voices and the sweet smell of porter surrounded them. They found a booth, and flung themselves into it. Benjamin skipped over to the counter. At times like this Charles felt himself to be a deeply historical personage. Every movement and gesture he made had already been endlessly repeated in this place. The low murmur and the sweet smell of drink were the past itself, covering him and laying claim to him. He could say nothing that had not been uttered before. 'I weep at cradles and I smile at graves. Your good health, Ben.' He took the pewter mug from his colleague and swallowed a great draught of ale. 'I drink this in the line of duty.'

'Of course.' Tom Coates raised his mug. 'Sheer necessity. No pleasure to be found in it.'

'I salute my fate.' Benjamin joined his mug with theirs.

'Ah yes. The Fates. The sisters. Hail, Atropos!' Charles finished the drink, and looked around for the waiter. He was always known as 'Uncle', a solemn old man who still wore knee-breeches and worsted stockings. 'Your finest, Uncle, when you are free.'

'Anon, sir. Anon.'

'That will be put on his gravestone,' Charles murmured to the others. 'Anon, sir. Anon. God will give up on him.'

The three sat drinking for an hour or more. They would not have been able to remember what they said. It was the experience of talking together that enlivened and reassured them, the linking of voice with voice, the call and the response, the sympathy of feeling. Charles had forgotten that he was supposed to meet William Ireland that evening. Eventually he left them at the corner of Moorgate, where they walked north towards Islington; he turned towards Holborn and home.

Then suddenly he was struck with a savage blow on the neck. 'What have you got? Give it to me.' He heard the voice and turned, but he was struck again. He staggered against the wall, and felt someone rifling through his pockets. His watch was ripped from its chain and his purse lifted quickly, almost impatiently; then he heard the thief running away, his footsteps echoing down the tall sides of Ironmonger Lane. He leaned against the wall by the corner and, with a sigh, sat down upon the stones. He reached for his watch, and then remembered that it had been taken; he realised that he had suffered no serious injury, but suddenly he was very tired. He was exhausted. He had become one of the whole host who had been assaulted on the same spot – the corner of Ironmonger Lane and Cheapside – and who had decided to sit upon the ground. The echo of footsteps, running from the scene, could still be heard.

Chapter Three

William Ireland sat with his father in the dining-room above the bookshop. Samuel Ireland's companion, Rosa Ponting, sat with them. 'That was a nice bit of perch,' she said. 'Very soft with the butter.' She dipped her bread into the last remnants of the butter sauce. 'I do believe it will rain. Sammy dear, will you pass me that potato? Did you know they came from Peru?'

She had lived in this house for as long as William could remember; she was now in middle age, and had acquired an extra chin, but she had preserved her youthful manner. She had once been what was known as a 'charmer', and still exercised all her claims to that title. 'You never will guess who stopped me in the street this morning. Why, it was Miss Morrison! I hadn't seen her for an age, you know. And I swear it was the same bonnet. I really do.' Samuel Ireland was staring ahead of him, lost in some troubled thought. His son could barely conceal his impatience. 'She invited me to tea on Tuesday week.' She sounded defiant. She had a right to speak, did she not? 'Now, William, I see you wish to leave the table. Please do.'

He looked at his father, who made no sign. 'May I go now, Father?'

'What? Yes. By all means.'

'I have something to show you.'

'What is it?'

'A surprise.' William rose from the table. 'On the shelves.' By this he meant the shop beneath them, although he had learned never to use that particular word in his father's presence. 'It is a gift. Something you have greatly desired.'

'Desire is a beast, William. Never desire too much.'

'But I presume this will be acceptable to you.'

'Some volume?' Samuel Ireland glanced at Rosa Ponting, who was not interested in such matters, and muttered, 'I leave you to your potato, Rosa.'

He followed his son down the plain deal staircase separating the bookshop from the house.

William took a parchment from one of the shelves and laid it upon the wooden counter. He was looking at it with evident delight. 'What is it, do you think?'

Samuel Ireland stroked the paper with the tip of his finger. 'A deed. From the time of the first James, at a guess.'

'Look more closely, Father.'

'Look at what, in particular?'

'The witnesses might interest you.'

Samuel Ireland took a pair of reading spectacles from the pocket of his jacket. 'No. It cannot be.'

'It is.'

'Where did you find this?'

'In the curiosity shop off Grosvenor Square. It was tied with other deeds. I broke the string, and this fell upon the floor. As soon as I retrieved it, I noticed the signature.'

'How much was it?' He asked the question very quickly.

'A shilling.'

'A shilling well spent.'

'It is yours, Father. It is a gift.'

'It is a thing I have dreamed of.' He took off his spectacles and wiped them with his handkerchief. 'The name and hand of William Shakespeare. It is the most remarkable document I have ever seen.'

'There can be no doubt about it?'

'No doubt at all. I have seen Shakespeare's own will in the library of the Rolls Chapel. Do you see the sweeping stroke through the tail of the "p", with its added stroke to be read as "per"? Do you see the imperfect "k", and the "e" with the reversed loop? It is the genuine article.'

'Take him all in all,' he had once told his son as they sat together after breakfast. 'He is our true parent. Chaucer is the father of our poetry, but Shakespeare is the father of our stage. No one truly fell in love before Romeo and Juliet. No one understood jealousy before Othello. Hamlet, too, is a great original.' He got up from his chair and strode over to the chimney-piece in the dining-room, where there was a small bust of Shakespeare carved out of mulberry wood. He had bought it in Stratford-upon-Avon, six months before. 'Yet the people of his uncultivated time never understood his genius. The plays were not fully published until after his death, and the texts themselves are so corrupted that many passages make no sense whatever. Some plays have simply disappeared.'

'Disappeared? Where?'

'Into the vast backward and abysm of time, as the bard would say. *Cardenio. Vortigern. Love's Labour's Won.* All gone.'

In the evenings, after supper, Samuel Ireland would sometimes read Shakespeare to his son. William could still recall the sensation of fog, or rain falling, just beyond the bay window of the shop-front. His father would sit with the oil lamp on the table behind him, casting the shadow of his head upon the open book as he intoned the words. '*How often when men are at the point of death they have been merry! Their keepers call it lightning before death.* How do you find that, Will? Magnificent!'

'He often mentions lightning. There is that line in *Romeo and Juliet* —'

His father was not listening to him. He was already searching for another passage with which to impress his son. He loved to recite the drama. He believed that he had a powerful voice, but to William it often sounded hollow and uncertain.

They had once travelled to Stratford 'in pursuit of the bard', as Samuel Ireland had put it. William knew that his father relished the opportunity of travelling away from home; in a temporary separation from the bookshop, and from the watchful presence of Rosa Ponting, he could occupy a more distinguished position in the world. One traveller in the Stratford coach had ventured to enquire, 'In what business are you engaged, sir?' Samuel Ireland had looked at him for a moment. 'I am engaged, sir, in the business of *living.*'

They had stayed that evening at the Swan Inn, Stratford, and on the following morning they had called upon Mr Hart, the butcher who shared Shakespeare's descent through the female line and who still lived on Henley Street in Shakespeare's own house. The scholar, Edmond Malone, had given Samuel Ireland a letter of introduction. Outside the old dwelling itself was a sign in black point. 'William Shakespeare was Born in this House. NB: a Horse and Taxed Cart to Let.'

'It is an honour, sir,' Hart had said when they entered the narrow passage of the house.

'The honour is mine, sir. To meet one of the family in these surroundings. My son, sir. William.' William shook his hand, which was warm and powerful. He imagined it around the neck of a hare or chicken. Ralph Hart was a short, bald man, of very pale complexion.

'I have no literary gifts, Mr Ireland. I am merely a tradesman.'

'But an honourable trade.' Samuel Ireland was very gracious. 'Was not the bard's father a butcher?'

'It is disputed. Some say he was a glover. But he kept cattle. Come into the parlour. Some like to call it the hall.' Hart seemed to William to be a composed and determined man; he was sure that he ran a thriving business. 'A dish of tea? I have no wife, but a very good housemaid.'

'Invaluable, sir, I am sure.'

It was for William Ireland the strangest sensation – to be in the house where William Shakespeare was reputed to be born, to be sitting in a room through which he had walked a thousand times, to see in the face of this butcher some lineaments of his illustrious family. And yet to feel nothing, to sense no familiar presence, to be stripped of all enchantment – that was most mysterious of all. He blamed his own incapacity. A more sensitive person would no doubt have thrived in this redolent atmosphere. A finer spirit would have been stirred, as if by a trumpet. But he registered nothing. The house was empty.

'You have heard of our latest discovery, Mr Ireland? His father's will was found hidden behind a rafter in this house. In the attic, where I keep my old pans.' William looked up, and noticed that the cross-beams of the parlour still displayed hooks for the haunches of meat.

'This is John Shakespeare's papist will, is it not?' Samuel Ireland lowered his voice slightly on the word 'papist'.

'Indeed it is.'

'Yet surely there must be some doubt, Mr Hart? Might it not possibly be forged by some fanatic?'

'Our friend, Mr Malone, believes it to be genuine. It is to be published in the *Gentleman's Magazine*.'

William noticed a faint flush in the butcher's pale face, and found himself addressing his father. 'Why should it be a forgery, Father?'

'There are some people, William, who might like to claim the father of the bard as one of their own.'

'I am too plain, I suspect.' Ralph Hart helped his guests to more tea. 'I believe what I see.'

William Ireland laughed. 'I see what I believe.'

Then he noticed that his father was looking oddly at him. He had somehow managed to say the wrong thing, and he felt abashed. He would do anything to please his father. He felt that in some way he had disappointed him, and that he must make amends. How he had disappointed him, he was not sure. It was some general failure. He worked in his father's business; he was his companion on various bookish expeditions. Yet sometimes he found his father looking at him in surprise, precisely as he had done in Mr Hart's parlour, as if he had just discovered that he was part of the household. William Ireland had never known his mother. His father had once told him that she had died when he was quite a baby, but nothing more was said. It was a subject not to be discussed. Rosa Ponting had shared his father's bed for many years, but William treated her with neither affection nor intimacy. His love was reserved for his father.

'So it is real, Father? It is genuine?' They were standing over the small parchment, peering at the scrawled signature.

'It is an authentic deed of the time. There can be no doubt about it.'

'Then if you have no doubts, I beg you to accept it as a gift from son to father.'

'Will you take nothing in return, Will? Here is my key. Have any volume you desire.'

'No, sir. I can accept nothing. It would taint the purity of the gift.'

'Of course this is not to be sold.' The idea of selling the document had never occurred to William. 'You should go back to that curiosity shop. Look in its corners. Summon forth its mysteries.'

They could hear Rosa Ponting coming down the stairs. 'Whatever are you two boys scheming? I'm sure I'll be the last to know.' It was her custom to consider Samuel Ireland still a 'boy'.

He looked warily at her as she entered the shop. 'Nothing whatever, dear.'

William could not bear to see her among the books and parchments. 'Father, I must deliver *Pandosto* before it grows too late.' He had already described Charles Lamb's purchase to his father.

'Leaving the house at this hour, William?' Rosa tapped her nose. 'I hope she is worth the effort.'

He had wrapped the volume in coarse brown paper, and now he took it down from the shelf as if he were using it as a shield against her; he left the shop quickly, muttering 'good night' into the air.

Laystall Street was only a short distance from the shop in Holborn Passage. And so, a few minutes later, Mary Lamb opened the door to him.

'I have an appointment with Mr Lamb.' He was afraid that he had sounded too fierce, and took a step backwards. 'Forgive my intrusion.'

'Do you mean Charles? Charles is not here.'

Her face was in shadow, the oil lamp in the hall shining behind her, but William was drawn to the sweetness of her voice. 'I have brought a book for him.' On an impulse he held it out to her. 'He purchased it this morning.'

'What is it?'

'*Pandosto.*'

'Greene's *Pandosto*? Oh do come in.' He hesitated on the threshold. 'My parents are with me in the drawing-room.' He followed her through the hall, and noticed the rich bronze of her untidy hair. Then he found himself in a small over-heated room, where an old couple were looking up at him in surprise. The man was eating toast, and there was butter on his chin. 'My name,' he said, 'is Ireland. William Henry Ireland.'

They said nothing. They stared at him so strangely that he might have come from the Sahara or the Antarctic wastes.

'Mr Ireland has brought Charles a book, Pa.'

Mr Lamb waved his toast at him and laughed. Mrs Lamb was not so merry. She did not like surprises of any kind, let alone one in the shape of a red-haired young man bearing books at eight o'clock in the evening. 'Charles is not with us, Mr Ireland. He is engaged.'

'Yet he asked me to bring him this.'

'Do let me look.' Mary took the parcel from him, and unwrapped it.

'The secret is in the inscription, Miss.'

She opened the book at its frontispiece, and repeated the words silently to herself. It was then he noticed the scars upon her face; the pits and ridges of her cheeks were caught in the candle-light. He looked away, and seemed to be studying the miniatures and cameos displayed on the walls of the little room.

'Why, this is a treasure, Mr Ireland. It was once owned by William Shakespeare, Ma.'

'That was a very long time ago, Mary.' So her name was Mary. 'I wonder at your brother buying such things when he has scarcely money enough for a pair of boots.' Mrs Lamb turned back to the toast now burning on the fork.

'Did my brother promise to pay you this evening, Mr Ireland?' She asked him this in a low voice so that her mother could not hear, and for an instant there was collusion between them.

'It was not much –'

'How much?'

'He owes two guineas only. One has been paid.'

'Would you excuse me for a moment, Mr Ireland?'

As Mary left the room Mrs Lamb looked at William intently. 'Has Charles purchased this book from you, Mr Ireland? Come back to the fireside, Mr Lamb.' Her husband had wandered over to William, and was brushing the dust and detritus from his jacket.

'Not exactly.' William hesitated, confused by Mr Lamb's attentions. 'We agreed –'

'Then I would be obliged if you would take this book away with you.'

'Oh no.' Mary hurried back into the room. 'This is a sacred book, Ma. Shakespeare himself turned its pages. Will you not sit with us for a moment, Mr Ireland?' She came up to him, and slipped two guinea coins into his hand. 'Will you take something with us?'

'I am sure Mr Ireland has better things to do with his time.' Mrs Lamb was not inclined to be hospitable, but the loud laughter of her husband seemed to tip the balance against her.

'There is port wine in the parlour, Ma. Mr Ireland is our guest.'

He could scarcely refuse to stay now and, in any case, he felt curiously at ease in Mary's presence. He sensed that she was innocent of the conventions. She was Charles Lamb's sister, too, and might provide another means of gaining his acquaintance.

'It was clever of Charles to find it. To find you, I should say.'

'He often passes by.' He had observed Charles on several occasions, staring in the window at the volumes on display. 'He came in this morning for the first time.'

'You must be the bookshop in Holborn Passage! Charles

has often mentioned it. I envy you terribly, being among such things. Mr Ireland owns a bookshop, Ma.'

'My father owns it —'

'Do you have a thriving trade?' Mrs Lamb had suddenly become more interested.

'Thriving is wiving.'

'Not now, Mr Lamb. Are you an old firm?'

'My father has continued the business for many years.'

Mary Lamb was turning over the pages of *Pandosto*. 'This is a book,' she said to him, 'for winter evenings.'

'Yes, Miss Lamb. With the world shut out.'

She kept her head bowed. 'This may have been the very book he read before *The Winter's Tale*.'

'He read it like a boy gazing on a beach, looking for pretty shells.'

She glanced up at him, astonished. 'Have you always loved Shakespeare?'

'Oh yes. When I was quite a child, I used to recite him. My father taught me the words.' William could recall the evenings when he stood upon a table, singing out in a clear calm voice the soliloquies of Hamlet and of Lear. He had been considered to be something of a prodigy by Samuel Ireland's friends.

'Charles and I would play the parts, too.' While her parents busied themselves about the dying fire, she told him how she and her brother would take on the roles of Beatrice and Benedick from *Much Ado About Nothing*, or of Rosalind and Orlando from *As You Like It*, or of Ophelia and Hamlet. They had the words by heart, and would furnish them with all the actions and attitudes that they deemed to be appropriate. As Ophelia Mary would turn away and weep; as Hamlet Charles would stamp his foot and scowl. For her these scenes seemed more real, more serious, than anything that happened to her day by day. 'But, for Charles, I believe they were part of a game. Now I am talking too much.'

'Not at all. It interests me exceedingly. You might like to know, Miss Lamb, that I have discovered his signature.'

'What do you mean?'

'That of Shakespeare. It is an old title deed from the reign of James. My father has authenticated it.'

'Is it certainly his hand?'

'There can be no doubt about it.' He noticed how the scars upon her face were a shade whiter than her living skin. 'I found it in a curiosity shop. In Grosvenor Square.'

'To possess such a thing –'

'It has often occurred to me that there must be some store of Shakespeare's papers. The contents of his study and his library have simply disappeared. They are mentioned in no will. Yet his family would have reverenced them.'

'Naturally.'

'They would have been preserved.'

'In Stratford?'

'Who knows where, Miss Lamb?' He sensed some intimacy between them. He did not know from where it had come; it had, as it were, descended upon them. Mary's father had started singing some old song.

'I have often wondered,' she said, as loudly as she dared, 'how Shakespeare would have appeared. In life, I mean.'

'No doubt he was very sane.'

'There is no question of that. Singularly sane.'

'He would have been open, and generous. And honest.'

'He had a spring in his step. No force could keep him down.'

'Of course not. He had that within him —' William's voice rose higher, but then he faltered. 'As you say, Miss Lamb, he was not an ordinary mortal.' The room suddenly seemed to him to be smaller; he had a definite sense of proximity to Mary, and to her parents, even to the miniatures upon the walls.

'Yet he understood what it was to be ordinary, Mr Ireland, don't you think?'

'He understood what it was to be anything.'

'There are ordinary people in his plays. There are nurses and prisoners and citizens. But they are ordinary to the point of genius.' He recognised Mary's loneliness even as she spoke to him; there was so much fervour within her that it could not often have been expressed. 'Think of Juliet's nurse,' she was saying. 'She is the essence of all nurses that have been or ever will be.'

'And then there is the porter in *Macbeth*.'

'Oh yes. I had forgot him. We must make a list of Shakespeare's ordinaries.' 'We' sounded familiar, and she turned at once to her mother. 'Wherever can Charles be, Ma?'

'Where he should not be, I imagine.' She took up her needle-work with a satisfied sigh of displeasure. Her husband had fallen asleep by the smouldering fire.

'May I play something for you, Mr Ireland? It will prove a point.' Mary went over to the small piano, in an alcove beside the fireplace, and opened its lid. When she began to play, her fingers scarcely seemed to touch the keys; but the notes of Clementi filled the drawing-room. She continued for a minute, and then turned towards him. 'It is pretty, don't you think? It is exalted. But it gives you no particular meaning. That is how I think of Shakespeare. He is purely expressive. He uses the black and the white. That is all.'

If tears had come into his eyes at that moment, he would not have known the reason. 'Will you play some more?'

The music passed over her parents without eliciting any response. But he was excited by it. There was no music in the bookshop; he knew only the tunes of the pleasure gardens and the inns. This was altogether different. It came from another sphere. It sustained his perception of Mary.

There was suddenly a banging at the door. Mary swiftly rose from the piano and went into the hall. Mr Lamb woke up and asked his wife, 'How many more sacks to the mill?'

William suddenly felt himself to be a stranger in the house. He had become an unwelcome visitor. He could hear the voices in the hall.

'I have lost my keys, dear.'

'What has happened to you?'

'I was hit.'

'Hit?'

'The ruffian took my watch and fled. Look at my head. Is it bleeding?'

Mrs Lamb looked wildly at William, and rose from her armchair. 'Whatever is the matter with you, Charles?'

'I have been robbed, Ma.' Charles came into the room and, to William, he seemed triumphant. 'Oh Mr Ireland. I quite forgot. Delighted to meet you again. As you can see, I have been detained.'

'Are you hurt, Charles?'

'No, Ma. I don't believe so. Have you seen the book, Mary?'

'What has been taken from you, Charles?'

'My watch, Ma. Nothing beside.'

Mary went over to her mother. 'It is nothing. Charles is quite well. Compose yourself.' She settled her back into the armchair. 'He is not marked. Only his watch has gone.' Mr Lamb had begun to doze again.

Charles sat down beside William. 'I was dining with friends. Otherwise I would have remembered our engagement. And then it happened.' There was, perhaps, a trace of condescension in his voice.

'It is of no consequence, Mr Lamb. Your parents and your sister have been most hospitable. We heard some music. Are you sure you are perfectly well?'

Charles brushed away the question with a movement of his hand. 'Music? You have been fortunate. This is the book, of course.' He took up the copy of *Pandosto* from the side-table where Mary had left it.

'The same.'

'May I?'

'It is yours now. Your sister has paid the residue.'

'And how did she do that?'

'I have no notion.'

'I do. Our great-aunt left her a small annuity. She picks it up from the West Lothian Bank in Seething Lane. Precious place.'

'You were fortunate, Charles.' Mary had quietened her mother, and now joined them. 'You could have been injured.'

'I am always lucky in the London streets, Mary. I lead a charmed life in the city.'

'Do you think he is wise, Mr Ireland?'

'If that is his experience. Some find it more testing.'

William had been walking, some months before, by the bank of the Thames just down from the Strand; it was high tide, at three o'clock in the morning. He often came at this time to savour the sound and the flow of the rising water. It gave him hope. He had seen a man standing by the edge, taking off his boots and trousers. There could be no doubt about his intention. 'Stop a minute.' William, acting on instinct, rushed over to him. 'Wait!'

He was young, no older than William himself. He was trembling with the cold. He muttered something William could scarcely hear; it seemed to be a passage from the New Testament, but William could not be sure. William took the young man's arm, but was shaken off. 'Take a look at my face,' the man said. 'You will never see this face again.' Then he seemed to hop backwards. He fell into the water and floated for a moment; as he floated, he smiled at William. Then he was gone. The strong tidal current of the Thames, below the quiet surface, sucked him down. It was so sudden, and so effortless, that William felt a curious desire to follow him.

He could still recall the sensation, as he sat with Charles and Mary Lamb in Laystall Street.

'I have prolonged my welcome,' he said, rising to his feet. 'My father will be expecting me.'

'But you will come again?' She turned to her brother. 'Mr Ireland has promised to show me more Shakespeare. The genuine hand.'

William left quietly, so as not to wake their father, and stood with Charles on the doorstep.

'Who was it who squared you? A pad?'

'I never saw him.' Charles held on to the door, as if he were now very tired.

'You had been drinking?'

'I am afraid so.'

'You must take care, Mr Lamb.' He was aware that he was taking Mary's part. 'The streets are never safe at night.'

'Whenever I think of the night, Mr Ireland, I think of cats in courtyards.'

Chapter Four

Three weeks after the events of that night, Mary Lamb decided to venture into Holborn Passage. Ever since their encounter she had often pictured to herself William Ireland among his books, and in her imagination he had already become a figure of some interest. Charles's friends were altogether too loud; they were too talkative. William was more sensitive. He had greater refinement of spirit, or so she supposed. She began to breathe more rapidly as she approached the bookshop and read the sign – 'Samuel Ireland, Bookseller' – hanging above the door. She passed the bay window and had decided quickly to walk on when a loud laugh, like a bellow, came from within. She paused and turned, to see an elderly man clapping William on the back while another man looked on. William glanced up at her, as if he had been awaiting her arrival, and then hurried to the door.

'Miss Lamb, will you come in? You have caught us in a white minute.' She was drawn into the shop almost against her will; she disliked meeting strangers. She recognised Samuel Ireland from the resemblance to his son but, in a hot flurry of embarrassment, she found herself shaking hands with the elderly gentleman who still had the remnants of his laugh upon his face.

Samuel Ireland was already talking to her. 'Honoured to make your acquaintance, Miss Lamb. Mr Malone has introduced himself, I see. You know of his scholarship, no doubt. What we have found, Miss Lamb, is a jewel.'

'More precious than any jewel, Father.'

'Do you see this?' Samuel Ireland held up a disc of red wax, slightly discoloured around its edge. 'It is his seal.'

'It is his device,' the old man said.

'So you have explained, Mr Malone.' Samuel Ireland was still smiling at Mary, but she did not care for his triumphal air. 'It bears repetition, sir, if you would be kind enough.'

He held out the seal for Mary's inspection, and Malone leaned over her to point out its details. She could smell the sourness of his old breath. 'This is the quintain.' Mary could see a pole, with a sack on one end, suspended across a bar. 'It is an instrument of jousting which turned and turned about. The rider would gallop towards it. He would strike it with his javelin or it would hit him. Do you understand the significance? I did not catch your name. "Shake" "spear" at it. And look there. There are the initials.' Mary could make out an indistinct 'W' and 'S' at the base of the seal. Now she understood their high spirits.

'He would have used it for correspondence,' William said. 'For theatre documents. Mr Malone has been kind enough to identify it for us. He has published a concordance of the plays.'

Malone was wearing a waistcoat of bright green silk, from which he took out a small bound paper notebook, and turned towards William's father. 'We need more than the object itself. We need the *fons et origo*, Mr Ireland.'

'Sir?'

'The provenance. The origin.'

Samuel Ireland looked at his son who, as Mary observed, quickly shook his head. 'We are not at liberty, Mr Malone —'

'A client?'

'I cannot say.'

'Well, I am sorry for it. The source of these treasures should be known.'

Samuel Ireland, apparently ignoring Malone's remark, took Mary's arm. 'Have you seen the deed, Miss Lamb?'

'The deed?'

'I have merely mentioned it to her, Father.'

'Oh this will never do. Miss Lamb really must see the deed. William tells me that you are a lover of all things Shakespearian.'

'Indeed. Yes, I am.'

'And here it is.' Mary was startled to discover that William's father had the faintest air of a cheap-jack. It was not how she had imagined his family. 'This is the thing, Miss Lamb.' He laid out a piece of vellum, and gently touched it with his forefinger. 'Very choice.'

'I have examined it carefully,' Malone told her. His mouth was once more perilously close. 'It is the exact handwriting. There can be no doubt about it.'

'I am very pleased,' was all she could think of saying.

William noticed her embarrassment. 'May I walk a little way with you, Miss Lamb?'

'Oh yes. Of course.'

After hurried farewells he took her out into the welcome chill of Holborn Passage.

'I am sorry to have disturbed you,' he said. 'They are enthusiasts.'

'Do not apologise, Mr Ireland. There is nothing wrong with enthusiasm. I merely felt the want of air.'

They walked in silence past an artificial-flower maker, whose stall always stood at the corner of Holborn Passage and King Street.

'I have a confession to make to you, Miss Lamb.'

'To me?'

'I told you that the deed came from a curiosity shop in Grosvenor Square. It did not. It came from the person who gave me the seal.'

'I don't see —'

'— what it has to do with you? Of course it has nothing to do with you. I will say no more about it.'

'No. I mean, why this person should have imparted such precious gifts.'

'Can I tell you a story, Miss Lamb? A month ago I was sitting in the coffee shop on Maiden Lane. Do you know the one? It has a very fine counter of French mahogany. I had taken with me an old black-print edition of Chaucer's *Canterbury Tales* which I had just purchased from a customer in Long Acre, and I was turning its pages when I heard a voice distinctly addressing me. "Do you know the virtues of books, sir?"

'It was a woman of middle age, sitting at a table behind me. She was dressed entirely in black with a black bonnet, a black shawl and a black umbrella. It is not usual for a woman to be sitting alone in a coffee shop, not even on Maiden Lane, and of course I was a little perturbed. She was clearly not a lady of the town. Excuse my indelicacy, Miss Lamb. Her age and appearance rendered that out of the question. And I surmised that she was either drunk or out of her wits. "Virtues, madam?"

' "Do you understand these things? Papers and books and suchlike?"

' "It is my profession."

' "I do not trust the lawyers." I noticed that she was drinking a cup of sassafras, a concoction I heartily detest. "As you can see, I am a widow."

' "I am sorry."

' "There is nothing to be sorry for. He was a brute. But he has left me many papers." Naturally I became interested. "I have no mind for papers. I need a mind." It occurred to me again that she might be one of those deluded women who are often to be found on the streets of London. But there was a carefulness, and steadiness, about her that suggested otherwise. "You may think it odd, sir, that I should address you in this way. But, as I said, I have an aversion to attorneys and law-beagles and suchlike. For the last several weeks I have said to myself – if I chance upon a person who has skills in studying and deciphering, then I will pounce upon that person." I could not help but smile at this. "You see, sir, that I am not used to flowery speech. Will you tell me your name?" She opened her purse of black silk, and I distinctly scented violets. It is a lovely perfume, don't you think? "I have no card. I have only my husband's. But the address is the same." I noted that her husband, Valentine Strafford, had been an importer of tea and that he had lived at a good address – Great Titchfield Street, in the parish of Marylebone. So I gave her my name, and promised to call upon her. It is what politeness required.

'Quite by chance I passed the house three days later on my way to a book-binder in Clipstone Street. Do you know the neighbourhood, Miss Lamb? It is not antique, but it is interesting. I had as yet no real intention of visiting her, but I must admit that I had been a good deal intrigued by her. I glanced into the ground-floor window and, on a long table, what did I see but heaps of papers and rolls of manuscripts! There were files and boxes on the table, also, together with other documents that had been tied with string or tape. So she had been speaking no less than the truth about her husband's papers. I did not hesitate, but on an instinct climbed the steps and rang the bell; to my surprise, she answered the door herself. "I hoped that you would come, Mr Ireland. I have been waiting for you."

'She took me into the ground-floor room that had the papers. I could see a long and narrow garden at the back, where there was one of those follies in the form of a rock-pool. They have become quite a fashion. "I am not sure, Mrs Strafford, if I will be able to help you."

'"Nonsense. I saw your eyes widen when you came into the room. You love such things." She offered me sassafras, but I declined. She obviously did not care for her husband's tea. "Of course you will be remunerated."

'"Before we speak of payment, let me browse for a while."

'"They may signify nothing."

'"They may signify a great deal. Let me examine them first."

'And so I set to work. It was an interesting collection. There were records of payments from Bermondsey Abbey, dating from the thirteenth century, and portions of a sixteenth-century rent-roll from the parish of Morebath in Devon. I hope I am not boring you. There was a map of the shoreline from Gravesend to Cliffe; the date was uncertain but, judging from the calligraphy, I guessed it to come from the middle of the seventeenth century. Of course I could not determine how any of these items had come into her husband's possession. I found a long inventory of goods signed by the Comptroller of the Excise at the London Customs House, dated in the thirteenth year of the reign of Richard II, as well as several pages of heraldic mottoes and devices. It seemed to me to be a random collection, but such a curious one that I felt a certain excitement. It appealed to my sense of adventure.

'Then I came across a deed, recently notarised and sealed with the distinctive green wax from the office of the sheriff of London. My father has pointed it out to me on several occasions. But this was no antiquity. It concerned a property in Knightrider Street, and it was clear from the document that Strafford had purchased a dwelling for £235 only two years before. I walked into the hallway and called out for Mrs Strafford, who came down at once from the first floor.

'"You have found something, Mr Ireland?"

'"I believe I have, Mrs Strafford. Let me show you this document. Have you seen it before?"

'"No. I have not."

'"Then you have a new house."

'"My husband never mentioned this. Whatever was he thinking? Knightrider Street? That is by St Paul's is it not? Not a cheap property, I am sure." She looked up at me, but I know nothing about such matters. "We must see it at once."

'We hailed a closed chaise. I prefer a cabriolet. These chaises smell of stale straw and damp umbrellas, don't you think? But there was nothing else to be had. We were stopped briefly in Holborn, where a young boy had been mangled by some horses, and then travelled eastward to Knightrider Street. Do you know that street, Miss Lamb? It curves like the side of a Roman amphitheatre. That is how it acquired its name.

'Mrs Strafford jumped out of the cab before I had a chance to pay the fare, and in her eagerness she walked ahead and passed the right door. I called her back, and we stood together in the street. It was a dark afternoon, and there was a candle behind the window. That was rather a surprise. It would not have seemed marvellous to me that the supposedly dead Strafford was living here and, judging by the look of horror upon Mrs Strafford's face, the same thought had occurred to her. But I could see her mustering her courage, and she mounted the steps to the door. She rapped upon it, and for the first time I noticed that she was not wearing gloves. Odd, don't you think? The candle was then removed by an unseen hand. We waited with growing impatience, until the door was opened by an old lady who seemed bowed by some frightful disease. "There is nobody at 'ome," she said.

'To my astonishment Mrs Strafford walked past her and called out "Come down! Come down!"

'"Mr Strafford never comes no more."

'"I beg your pardon?" Mrs Strafford had been about to climb the staircase, but she turned back.

'"He ain't bin 'ere for eight months or more. I ain't bin paid for two months neither."

'"You are the housekeeper, are you?"

'"I was, but I ain't bin paid."

'"We will attend to that." I could see that Mrs Strafford was not a woman for delay. "How much did my husband owe you?"

'If she was at all surprised by the sudden appearance of Mrs Strafford, she did not show it. "Sixty shillin's. Seven and six per week."

'"You don't mind paper money, I take it?" She took three pound notes from her purse. "It is as good as metal."

'There was some further conversation between them but I was curious to discover what, if anything, lay behind the doors of this old house. I love the evidence of the past, Miss Lamb. There was a back room, just beyond the staircase; as soon as I entered I sensed the faint odour of old papers, as refreshing to me as any herb or plant. What is the sweetness of flowers compared to the savour of dust and confinement? There was a large wooden bureau in a corner of the room; I opened it and discovered piles of documents folded, tied, or laid down in single sheets.

'Mrs Strafford came up suddenly behind me. "What is this? More papers? Oh Lord, my husband was drowning in papers."

'"They may be all over this house. What can I do –"

'"What can you do with them? You can keep them, Mr Ireland. You found the house for me. You may have its papers."

'I reflected for a moment, and found myself looking out through a grimy window at a small paved courtyard. "No. That is not just. Let us put it differently. If I find anything that is of value to me, but not to you, then I may keep it."

'"Agreed."

'"As easily as that?"

'"It is easy to give away what I never possessed. Here are the housekeeper's keys, Mr Ireland. When you have finished your work, the house will be sold."

'I came back to Knightrider Street on the following morning, with the excuse to my father that I was examining a gentleman's library in Bow Lane. As I said to you, I wished this to be my own adventure. I began at the top of the house, and inspected each room thoroughly. The house was for the most part bare of furniture, except for a small room that the ancient house-keeper had occupied, but there were several chests and cases in which I found more documents. It was clear to me now that Mr Strafford had been an inveterate and eager collector of manuscripts; there were bills of mortality, actors' parts written on long scrolls, diplomatic correspondence and even folio pages from an illuminated Bible. Do tell me if I am boring you, Miss Lamb. It was on the second morning, however, that I discovered the deed that contained the signature of William Shakespeare. The deed my father has just shown to you. I had not noticed the name at first, and had put the document to one side with some other deeds. Yet something must have caught my attention. It may have been no more than the proximity of the "W" and the "Sh". I picked up the page again and, an hour later, I was conveying it back to the bookshop. It was the perfect gift for my father. But then, just yesterday, I also found the seal.'

'Does the woman know of the seal?' Mary had listened in profound silence to his story, but was now very curious.

'Mrs Strafford? Oh yes. But she does not value it. She is not in the least interested in Shakespeare. She lacks our – enthusiasm.'

'Her husband did not.'

'I am not yet sure whether he collected these things out of deliberation, or whether he amassed material injudiciously. I still have to search many boxes and cases. I felt obliged to tell my father about Strafford's papers, but I have given him no details. He would be indiscreet. I know him.'

'I envy you.'

'Whatever for, Miss Lamb?' No one had ever addressed him in that fashion.

'You have a quest. A purpose.'

'I would not put it as highly as that.'

'Oh, I would.'

'Then perhaps I can share this – this quest – with you.'

'In what way?'

'I can bring my discoveries to you. They will please my father, and they will also please you.'

'Would you do that?'

'Of course. Willingly. Gladly. And of course you may tell your brother.'

They had walked as far as Catton Street, but they seemed reluctant to part. So Mary walked back with him down High Holborn. She had the strangest interest in him – as she put it to herself – but she was quite at a loss to explain the reasons for this. She sensed that he had no mother but, again, she could have given no explanation; it was his intensity, perhaps, that suggested some inner unease. She remarked later to her brother that he had 'lonely eyes', and Charles laughed at her sentimentality; but, for her, it was an exact description.

'Lonely is not far from lovely,' he said.

'Be serious, Charles.' There was some colour in her cheeks. 'He needs protecting.'

'From what?'

'I am not sure. There seems to be some battle between himself and the world. He believes himself to be the injured party, and he will keep up the fight.'

Chapter Five

When William Ireland returned to the bookshop, having left Mary Lamb at the corner of High Holborn and watched her disappear into the crowd, he found his father alone. Samuel Ireland was walking backwards and forwards, his patent-leather shoes rapping upon the wooden floor.

'Mr Malone sends his compliments. He had to leave for an appointment with his oculist.'

'He was pleased, was he not?'

'Delighted. Beyond measure.' He walked the length of the shop before turning to his son. 'When do you next see your patron?'

William had not related to him as much as he had told Mary Lamb; he had informed his father only that he had found the deed to a house in the library of an elderly lady who, in return, had given him permission to keep certain items which were of no interest to her. They were, as far as she was concerned, 'mere paper'. He also described to him how he had sworn a solemn oath never to reveal her name. William knew his father to be excitable, grandiloquent and liable to spin extravagant schemes. It had been his father's sudden impulse, for example, to bring in Edmond Malone.

'I said that I would call upon her in a few days.'

'A few days? Do you know what we have here?'

'A seal.'

'A mine. A mine of gold. Do you know the price at auction of such things?'

'I have never considered it, Father.'

'I presume your patron does not, either, or she would not put them at your disposal. Or shall I call her your benefactor?' If there was a tone of irony in his voice, William refused to notice it. 'She is above such things, is she?'

'They are simply a gift. As I told you, I found a deed to her late husband's house —'

'And they have no monetary worth for you?' Samuel Ireland resumed his pacing about the shop. It was clear to William that he was possessed by some strange energy, or vigour, which he did not try to conceal. 'Let me ask you this, William. Do you have it within you to improve yourself? To succeed in this life?'

It was a challenge, not a question. 'I hope so. I presume so.'

'Then you must seize your opportunity. I am convinced that there will be more Shakespearian papers. To find a deed, and a seal, in one place is beyond mere coincidence. You must seek them out, William.' He turned his back, in order to rearrange some books upon a shelf. 'Your patron need not know. We can sell them privately.'

William noticed a white hair on the back of his father's jacket, and resisted the urge to brush it away. 'They cannot be sold, Father.'

'Cannot?'

'I will not profit from her generosity.'

His father made a visible effort to stand more upright. 'You will not consider my opinions – my feelings – in this?'

'Of course I will always be willing to listen to your advice, Father, but for me this is a principle.'

'You are young to talk of principles.' His back was still turned. 'Do you think your principles will gain you a better life?'

'They will not get me a worse one.'

'Do you wish to work in a shop for the rest of your life?' His father turned round, but he still did not look at him. He went over to the counter, and wiped it with the palm of his hand. 'Have you no ambition beyond that of a tradesman?' William stayed silent, forcing his father to speak. 'If I had possessed this benefactor, this patron, when I was starting in the world, I would have taken advantage of it.'

'What advantage?'

'To climb higher.'

'And how would I achieve that, Father?'

'By putting money in the bank.' He looked at his son for that moment. 'Do you have any notion of what poverty is? I came into the world with empty pockets. I had to fight for my bread. I attended the free school in Monmouth Street. Well, I have told you about that.' William had indeed heard his father's story before. 'I begged and borrowed a few shillings to set up a stall in the street. I prospered very slowly, but I prospered. You know all this.'

'I do.'

'But do you know how to emulate it? Do you know how to begin?' Samuel Ireland climbed slowly up the staircase, pausing on one step as if he were short of breath.

William waited until he had disappeared into the room above. The he went over to the red seal of Shakespeare, took it in his hands, and began to weep.

Three days after this William came into the shop, whistling 'Sweet Julie', and ran upstairs to the dining-room. Rosa Ponting and his father were sitting by a sea-coal fire, drawing up a list of acquaintances to whom a Christmas posset might usefully and profitably be sent. 'Cummings is too old,' Rosa was saying. 'He will dribble it.'

'I have a gift, Father.' From his breast pocket he took out a sheet of faded vellum. 'A gift for all seasons.' Samuel Ireland rose quickly from his chair, and took the paper eagerly. 'It is his testament.'

'A testament, not a will?'

'Without a doubt. Did you not tell me once that he died a papist?'

Samuel Ireland went over to the table, and laid out the document. 'There was a suspicion of it. Nothing more.'

They had discussed the matter during their recent visit to Stratford. After they had left the birthplace, where they had drunk tea with Mr Hart, they had walked down Henley Street in the direction of the river. They were considering the will of John Shakespeare which had been concealed behind a rafter, and were speculating whether the son had followed the religious convictions of the father. Samuel Ireland had a jewel-topped cane, which he prodded on the ground for emphasis. 'There was a play on the papist Thomas More, which was supposed to be Shakespeare's. But it was a bastard issue.'

'A bastard issue? What is that, Father?'

They looked at each other for a moment, and Samuel banged his cane upon a cobble. 'It is a nothing. A mere term. It means that it is not part of the canon.'

William stared ahead, and did not even notice a small herd of piglets being driven down Henley Street. 'But it is an interesting expression. Bastard issue.'

'These phrases can be used too freely, William. Scholarship is not exact. Do you see those little creatures?'

'So the scholars may be wrong?'

'They give too much thought to sources. To origins. Instead of studying the wonderful sublimity of the bard's verses, they hunt for the originals Shakespeare may have copied. It is false learning.'

'There are some who say that Shakespeare copied everything.'

'That is exactly the conjecture I mean. It is absurd. It is nonsensical. He was a divine original.'

'That is to say, without origins?'

'Shall we say, William, that origins are of no consequence?'

'I am glad to hear it.' His father looked at him sharply for a moment. 'Shakespeare stands alone.'

Samuel Ireland was still studying the parchment laid out on the dining-room table.

'The testament proves that he was not a papist, Father. Can you make out the words?'

'There is something here commending his soul to Jesus.'

'There is no Mary. There are no saints. No superstition. No bigotry.'

Samuel Ireland wiped his eyes, with what seemed to be a nervous gesture. 'There is no mistake, William?'

'Look at the signature, Father. It is identical with that upon the deed.'

Rosa Ponting was still examining the list for the Christmas posset. 'It is a waste of your time, Sammy. If your son will not sell these things, what is the use of them?'

On a cold evening in the following week Samuel and William Ireland were invited into the library of Church House beside St Mildred's, Fetter Lane. Here they were greeted by Doctor Parr and Doctor Warburton, both of them identically dressed in clerical black with white stocks, white wristbands and dusted grey periwigs.

'Delighted,' said Doctor Parr.

'Immeasurably,' said Doctor Warburton.

They both bowed very gracefully.

'Mr Malone has written to the Archbishop.'

'The Archbishop is overjoyed.'

William was so intrigued by these two elderly clerics that he felt obliged to look away for a moment. He concentrated upon a print of Abraham and Isaac, surrounded by a heavy black frame.

'To know that our foremost poet has been freed of all suspicion of papistry. It is a great joy.'

William noticed, also, that both divines smelled of bruised oranges.

'Will you join us in an amontillado?' Doctor Parr asked them.

'The driest of the dry.'

Doctor Warburton rang a small bell and a black boy – dressed in black, also, with white wristbands and a grey periwig – brought in a silver tray with four glasses and a decanter. Doctor Parr poured the sherry and proposed a toast to the 'divine bard'.

Samuel Ireland then took from his carrying-case the document that William had brought back in triumph the week before. 'Can you read the Secretary hand, sir?'

'I have known it all my life.'

'Then this will cause you no difficulty.'

Doctor Parr took the vellum from him and handed it to his colleague. Doctor Warburton, putting on his spectacles in a ritual he clearly enjoyed, began to read aloud. 'Forgive us, oh Lord, all our sins and cherish us like the sweet bird that under the cover of her spreading wings receives her little brood and hovering over them keeps them – what is this word?'

He passed the paper to Doctor Parr. 'Harmless, Warburton.'

'– who keeps them harmless and in safety. Keep in safety, too, your sovereign James divinely appointed. This is excellent, Parr. He subscribed to our English Church. Note the image of the bird.'

William walked over to a window and looked down into Fetter Lane. There was a plaque on the wall there, beneath the elm tree, which read 'This Is Where the Great Fire of London Was Halted'. Hanging in this library, between the window and the shelves, was a tapestry depicting 'Jesus among the Doctors in the Temple'; there were some threads unravelled loosely from it and, on an impulse, he plucked them out and put them in his pocket. When he turned round he realised that the black servant had been observing him; the boy was shaking his head and smiling at him. Since the others were deeply intent upon examining Shakespeare's testament, William walked over to him. 'A memento,' he said. 'A memory of this place.'

The boy's eyes were large and tremulous. It was as if he were looking at William from under water. 'That is no concern of mine, sir.'

William was astonished at the purity of his diction. The boy might have been an Englishman. William's only previous contact with a Negro had been the crossing-sweeper by London Stone, who scarcely seemed able to speak at all. 'How long have you worked here?'

'Since I was a very small child, sir. I was brought across the ocean and redeemed here.' William did not quite know what the boy meant by 'redeemed' but it had some connotation of debt or purchase. And yet it might have meant that he had been baptised.

Joseph's mother, Alice, had taken him aboard a ship sailing from the Barbadoes with a cargo of sugar cane; Alice had recently become the captain's mistress, and had pleaded for her small son to join them on the journey to England. Joseph was then six years old. On their arrival at the Port of London the captain took mother and son to the Evangelical Mission for Seamen, on Wapping High Street, and ordered them to wait there for his return. They sat upon the steps all night.

The following morning Alice told Joseph to wait there for the captain while she went in search of food. She never returned. Or, rather, she had not returned seven hours later when Hannah Carlyle had found the young black boy curled up against the door of the Mission. 'Goodness me,' she asked no one in particular, 'what is it?' He knew only the Bajan patois of his country, and she did not understand what he answered. 'Bless you for your heathen tongue,' she said. 'Your skin is black, but your soul is white. You have been sent here for a purpose.'

The boy's colour caused little remark among the illegitimate white children of this neighbourhood, sailors' children who ran wild through the riverside alleys and warehouses of the docks. This was a strange world where it seemed to Joseph that the sea entered London. The wind was like a sea-wind, and the birds were sea-birds. The ropes, and masts, and barrels, and planks, gave him the impression of a ship upon land.

Yet Joseph was eventually taken out of Wapping by Hannah Carlyle, who gave him to her cousin who was the housekeeper of Church House in Fetter Lane. So he was brought up in the company of Doctor Parr and Doctor Warburton; they taught him English, and he acquired from them the slightly old-fashioned diction that had surprised William Ireland. The divines also took turns in entering his bed. Doctor Parr would suck his member and masturbate himself, whereas Doctor Warburton would simply fondle him before returning with a sigh to his own room.

'It may interest you to know, sir, that my name is Shakespeare. Joseph Shakespeare.'

William could not help smiling. 'How is that possible?'

'It was a name given to the unfortunate slaves, sir. It was a jest.'

Doctor Parr was reading aloud another part of the testament. 'Our poor weak thoughts are elevated to their summit and then, as snow from the leafless trees, drop and distil themselves till they are no more.' He wiped his lips with a white handkerchief tucked beneath his wristband. 'This should be read out from every pulpit in England.'

William walked over to them and, on the pretence of asking for the time, whispered in his father's ear. 'This will not be considered a bastard issue.'

'We have very fine passages in our church service,' Warburton was saying. 'And our litany abounds with beauties. But here is a man who has distanced us all. Genuine feeling breathes through the whole composition.'

'Is it in the style of Shakespeare?' William asked him.

'There can be no doubt about it. This must become known to the world.'

'I am intending to write an essay for the *Gentleman's Magazine*,' Samuel replied.

His son looked at him in astonishment.

There was time for more sherry, and a further toast to 'the bard' before Doctor Parr and Doctor Warburton took their visitors to the front door of Church House. 'It has been a privilege,' Parr said, 'to touch the paper upon which Shakespeare wrote.'

'It has been an honour, Mr Ireland.' Warburton looked down the Lane as if he were expecting an invading army. 'A solemn joy.'

As they crossed Fetter Lane, William grabbed his father's arm. 'I did not know you were writing an essay.'

'And why not?'

'You should have informed me, Father.'

'A father to ask permission from his son? Is that what you are saying?'

'You should have consulted me.'

'Consult? What is there to consult about? As the good Warburton has said, the news must be given to the world.'

In truth William had intended to compose his own article on the subject. From the day he had shown the first signature to his father, he had nurtured the ambition of writing biographical essays on Shakespeare. Shakespeare would be his key to publication. 'There may be others, Father, who can write.'

'There are no others acquainted with the subject as we are. Oh. Surely you don't mean yourself?'

William blushed. 'I have as good a claim as you.'

'You are a youth, William. You have no powers of composition.'

'How do you know that?'

'*Sensus communis.* Common sense. I know you.'

William was suddenly becoming very angry. 'You could not have said that to the young Milton. Or to Pope. Chatterton was my age when he died.'

'Milton and Pope were possessed by great genius. Surely you do not believe that you —'

'Well. I have *inherited* none. That is obvious enough.'

They did not speak for the rest of the evening.

In fact Samuel Ireland had already written to the editor of the *Gentleman's Magazine*, Philip Dawson, the week before.

Dawson was a shrewd man of business, quiet and steady,

but when he received Ireland's letter he had put his head back and whistled. 'This is a discovery,' he said. 'My word.'

He went over to a cabinet and took out a bottle of soda. He drank only soda so that, as he always said, his mind would remain clear and transparent. He was known to his acquaintances as 'Soda', and even signed his more familiar letters with that name. He had simply signed himself 'Dawson', however, in his response to Samuel Ireland. He had asked him to call.

As Samuel Ireland approached the offices of the *Gentleman's Magazine*, in St John's Gate at Clerkenwell, he felt for a moment his son's discontent. As soon as William had brought the first papers to him, Samuel had immediately seen the profit in them. There were scholars and collectors who would pay more than a modest sum for any signature or deed. The fact that William refused to sell them was of no great consequence; Samuel was sure that, over weeks or months, he could persuade him otherwise. No son of his could dismiss the prospect of financial gain. What concerned him most, as he walked towards St John's Gate, was the seriousness of his task. He was about to reveal to the English public a number of hitherto unseen and unknown Shakespearian articles. Samuel Ireland would then become the object of controversy. He was already wondering how he would be described – as a bookseller, a tradesman, a shop-owner? And how was it best to conduct himself in the company of scholars and men of letters?

Philip Dawson was sitting at a desk at the far end of a long, low room; it was above the gate-house itself, and its ceiling was supported by great timber beams of the fifteenth century. As soon as he saw Samuel Ireland he rose to his feet and walked towards him; he noticed at once the fashionable cut of the man's jacket, the florid complexion, the full mouth and the sharp, restless eyes. 'You have produced a wonder, Mr Ireland,' he said after their formal greeting. He was still gazing at him frankly.

'It *is* a wonder, Mr Dawson. May I have some water before we begin to speak?' His throat was very dry.

'Soda?'

'Perfectly acceptable.' He swallowed it down in large draughts, and could not disguise a burp when he put down his glass. 'Apologies.'

'Many of my guests do that. The soda shakes them up.'

'I am sure. I presume that you have read my letter?'

'All I require now is the evidence, Mr Ireland. The document itself.'

'By curious coincidence –' He reached down to his carrying-case and took out the testament of William Shakespeare which, for the sake of safety, he had wrapped in a linen handkerchief and placed in an envelope.

Dawson took it out and examined it carefully. 'It is a remarkable thing.'

'Very.'

'The sentiments are orthodox, of course.'

'It is a comfort, Mr Dawson. If our bard had been proved a puritan or a papist . . .'

'It would have thrown a strange light upon his dramas.'

'It would have been disquieting.'

'But will it be deemed authentic? That is the question.'

Samuel Ireland was surprised. He had taken for granted the

genuineness of the documents. For what possible reason would William's patron falsify them? 'I can assure you, sir, that they have an unsullied provenance. You may depend upon it.'

'I am glad to hear it. But we will need a palaeographer.'

'I beg your pardon?' Samuel Ireland had never heard the term.

'A palaeographer. A reader of ancient hands.'

'Mr Edmond Malone has already verified the signature.'

'Malone is a scholar. But he is not a palaeographer. Would you excuse me for a moment?' Dawson sat down at his desk and rapidly scrawled upon a card. 'Jane!' A young woman appeared in the doorway, clutching a wooden tray of metal type. 'Could you take this to Mr Baker? You know the address.' Jane interested Samuel Ireland. Her dark hair was neatly cut around her oval face, in the style known as 'Morocco', and she reminded him of the painting of Lady Keppel in Somerset House. 'Mr Baker is an authority on the sixteenth-century hand. I have asked him to call upon us. More soda?' Ireland accepted the glass of soda water, and drank it down quickly.

'You are quick, Mr Baker.'

Jonathan Baker was a short and stocky man with a countenance that expressed complete weariness. His mouth was turned down, and his eyes heavy. To Samuel Ireland he seemed like some Pantaloon out of the comic operas. He had arrived in the office wearing a 'morning glory', the name for a peaked hat of uncertain date.

'When I am summonsed by you, Mr Dawson, I fly.' His voice was light, almost playful. 'May I see this document?' He had not looked at Samuel Ireland, as if any greeting might prejudice his examination. He took the testament and held it up to the light from the window. 'The paper is good. The watermark is of the period. And the ink is very fine. Do you see how it has faded into the weave?' He had forgotten that he was still wearing his hat, and with an apology removed it. 'It is a good sixteenth-century hand. I have studied Shakespeare's signature in the past –'

'From where, sir?'

'His will is in the Rolls Chapel. It is beneath glass, Mr Dawson. But I studied it well.' He took from his pocket a strip of paper. 'I plotted it with a micromemnonigraph of my own invention.' On this paper were a series of lines and numbers. 'I have my own method of calligraphy, you see, which is based upon exact principles.'

His voice was so lively, and so graceful, that for a moment Samuel Ireland did not follow his meaning. But, as Baker studied the signature on the testament, he began to feel uneasy. What if this man should suspect some falsehood? Baker pored over it, his nose almost touching the vellum, with an occasional 'Oh!' and 'Aha!' 'There are some abnormalities,' he said eventually. 'But they are produced in certain circumstances. On the whole, I am inclined to believe it is the thing. The genuine article. Congratulations, sir.' He looked at Ireland for the first time. 'I presume you have brought this here?'

'I have that honour.'

'Then you have performed a great service.'

When Samuel Ireland eventually recounted this scene to his son, he imitated all the actions of Dawson and of Baker – how Baker had bowed to him, how Dawson had waved a soda-bottle in the air, and how Jane had cried 'Huzzah!' from the doorway. William at first seemed horrified when his father told him of the arrival of the palaeographer. By what right had this Dawson called in a stranger? But he had laughed out loud when his father had told him of the vindication.

'What else did you expect, Father?' he asked him. 'Who could possibly have doubted you?'

William left the room for a moment. He was wrapped in an elation so great that he did not wish to be seen.

Chapter Six

'What is "the mother"?' It was the first day of spring. Charles Lamb was sitting with Tom Coates and Benjamin Milton in the Billiter Inn. 'I read somewhere that Julius Caesar had "the mother". But I have no idea what it means.'

'Have you had your mother, Ben? Whoosh.' Tom was drinking 'Stingo' and could not resist sneezing on to his sleeve.

Benjamin patted him on the back. 'God bless you, dearest. I am surprised at you, Charles. Surely you recall that "the mother" is in *King Lear*. It is *hysterica passio*. The womb mounts higher and higher, in your frenzy, and suffocates the heart. And the womb is the mother.'

'But men have no wombs.'

'They have entrails, have they not? They can bleed.'

'My mother is always hysterical.' Tom finished the rest of

his drink, and put his arm in the air to signal that he wanted another. 'She cries at the drop of a stitch.'

'The passions create bodily humours.' Benjamin was intent upon following his thought through the mist of drink. 'And the lower vapours rise into the brain. That is hysteria.'

Charles was thinking of his sister.

A week before, Mary had been in the kitchen, preparing kidneys for that evening's supper, with her mother sitting beside her. 'I will never know,' Mrs Lamb was saying, 'why some people insist on devilling their kidneys. What is wrong with frying?' Mary cried out in pain. She had sliced the inside of her thumb, and the blood was seeping on to the wooden chopping board. Charles had been watching her cut the meat – watching her idly, incuriously – but he could have sworn that she had deliberately injured herself. She had gone from the kidney to the thumb with a calm movement of the knife. Mrs Lamb shrieked at the sight of the blood, and jumped up from the chair. She was about to take her daughter's hand but Mary turned away from her and found a piece of linen cloth in a drawer; she wound it around her thumb quickly, and looked at Charles. It seemed to him that she was triumphant.

Later that evening she had gone into his room, with the excuse that she wished him to translate a difficult phrase from Lucretius. She sat at the bottom of his bed. 'You know, Charles, I must get out of this house.'

'Why, dear?'

'Can't you see? It is killing me.' He was astonished. She noticed his astonishment, and burst into tears. He leaned towards her, but he did not touch her. She stopped crying as quickly as she had begun. She wiped her face with the cloth bandage around her thumb. 'I am deadly serious, Charles. I must leave or I will go insane.'

'What would you do? Wherever would you go?'

'That doesn't matter.'

Mary had never revealed these feelings to him before; they shocked, and unnerved, him. He could think of no reply. There was of course the implication that she was willing to leave him – to abandon him – but he dismissed this at once. There was no possibility of it. But the source of her anger and frustration was hidden from him. He had believed her to be contented, placid almost, in the company of her parents and in the comfort of familiar surroundings. She had time for her reading and for her sewing. Had she not said that she always looked forward to their conversations at the end of the day? He could not take her threat seriously. 'And what would become of Pa?' was all he said.

She looked at him wildly, and left the room. He could hear her steps upon the stairs, then the opening and closing of the front door. She had gone out without a shawl or bonnet.

The night was mild, but there was a strong wind blowing through the streets. Mary Lamb had no direction or purpose: she had to escape into the air. She was walking quickly across the cobbles. She saw a rat entering a water-pipe, but she felt no unease. It was the world. In the force of the wind pieces of orange-peel and scraps of newspaper were rustling over the stones; her hair was not pinned, and it blew about her neck and forehead. I am a witch, she thought, a midnight hag. I have become accursed. She started to run, and turned a dark corner. In her haste she fell against someone.

'Miss Lamb?'

For a moment she did not recognise him. 'Oh, Mr Ireland. I'm sorry. I have alarmed you.'

'Not in the least. No harm done whatsoever.' They looked at each other in silence for a moment. 'Is there anything the matter?'

'Matter? There is no matter.' In her anxiety, and embarrassment, she did not know what she was saying. 'Will you walk with me a little way?'

'Gladly.'

They walked down the street together, Ireland slightly ahead as if he were leading her forward. Then she laughed aloud. 'I must seem to be a dissolute woman, without a shawl. And my hair is undone.'

'Oh no. Nothing of the kind.'

They walked in silence, as she slowly recovered her composure. 'I like to watch the form and pressure of the wind,' she said at last. 'Do you see how it ripples across the windows there?' She felt protected by the close cover of the darkness in the city; she was comforted by the ash-coloured air. 'You are a lover of London, too, Mr Ireland.'

'How do you guess that?'

'Well, you have survived it.'

'I have survived.'

'And you walk in the night.'

'I cannot sleep. I am too excited.'

'May I ask the reason?'

'I was intending to call on you tomorrow with my discovery. This is not the time –'

'It is always time.'

'I can put the matter simply enough.' He put his face up

to savour the wind. 'I have found a poem by Shakespeare. A new poem. Unseen. Unread.'

'Can this be true?'

'All is true, Miss Lamb. I discovered it only last night, among the papers.'

'I would like to see it. At once.'

'Would you?'

'Oh yes.' It was a refuge from her misery. To dwell in another time – if only for a moment – offered her proof that she need not be confined or constricted. That was perhaps why she had run into the night.

'I have not carried it with me.' He was almost apologetic. 'I have it in the house.'

'May we go there please?'

'It is late. But if you take no offence –'

'Not the least in the world.'

So they walked the short distance to Holborn Passage. 'I did not know what it was until I examined it carefully. It was on a piece of manuscript that had been torn from a larger sheet.' William was talking quickly. 'The writing is very small, and at first I did not recognise it for what it was. It was not written in poetic form, you see, but in long lines. To conserve space. Then I noticed the peculiar style of the "s", and I remembered where I had seen it before. It was his hand, of course. Without any doubt.'

'And the poem concerns what?'

'It is a short complaint, as one lover might make to another. Please wait a moment, Miss Lamb.' They had arrived at the bookshop, which was in darkness. He unlocked the door, and a few moments later came back with a lamp.

'Well met by oil-light,' she whispered.

'Indeed. This is an adventure.' Yet, in the pale circle of the flame, he looked anxious and confused. 'My room is on the second floor. Please to be quiet. My father sleeps above me.' He led her up the panelled deal staircase, through the dining-room, and then upwards to a further storey. It was an old house, a sounding box of wood with uneven floors and curved timbers. He unlocked the door of his room, with two separate keys. When he put down the lamp she noticed that the walls were covered with sheets of engravings. Here were the heads of Shakespeare and of Milton, of Spenser and of Tasso, of Virgil and of Dante.

'Who is that?'

'That is John Dryden. The father of English prose.'

'A mighty position.'

'Or so my father says. Please do sit down, Miss Lamb. I am afraid there is little space.' With great care he took from a drawer a piece of manuscript paper. She observed now that there were several boxes and chests in this little room, taking up most of the available floor. She sat down upon one of them as in a hushed voice he began to read from the manuscript, the lamp illuminating the paper. She was aware of Mr Ireland sleeping in the chamber above their heads.

> 'Not a maid who in his purview came
> Could miss the force of his unerring aim
> What was once wild did soon become all tame
> And he did seize what once he wished to maim.
> And thus at once their virtue he forecloses
> Like hue and tincture taken from fair roses.'

He put down the lamp. 'That has the Shakespearian ring, does it not?'

'Who is there?' It was his father, calling from the floor above.

'Only me, Father. I am reading.'

'Be sure to extinguish the lamp.'

'Of course, Father.' He waited for a few moments, his eyes closed; it was as if he did not wish Mary to see them blazing. 'Does it strike you, then, as genuine Shakespeare?'

'Oh yes. It could be no one else.' She wanted to reinforce his excitement, to be caught up in his elation so that she might leave her own life behind.

'I have not told him anything as yet.' The motion of his head upwards signified whom he meant. 'He would take all the glory. If I wrote something on this discovery, and gave it to your brother, do you think he could have it published?'

'Of course he could. Charles would be delighted to do so. It would be his privilege.'

'Will you tell him from me, then, that I have begun to write it? I will present the essay in a week's time.' He seemed suddenly to become aware of the difficulty of their situation, sitting together in his bed-chamber. 'I think, Miss Lamb, that I should accompany you home.' His voice was very low and steady. 'I hope I have not offended you in any way.'

'Not at all, Mr Ireland. I have intruded on your hospitality, I am afraid.'

'The night and the wind entered our heads. We will leave as quietly as possible.'

So he took her out into Holborn Passage and then walked with her to Laystall Street. He stayed by her side until they reached her door, where she turned and smiled. 'It has been a remarkable evening.'

'And for me.'

Charles was standing in the hallway, his hair dishevelled, when she came in. 'Wherever have you been, Mary? I have been searching the streets.'

'I have been listening to Shakespeare.'

'I do not understand you.'

'William Ireland has found a poem. I have just heard it.'

'He read it to you in the street?'

'No. I returned with him to the bookshop.'

'In the middle of the night? Have you lost your senses?'

She looked at him for a moment as if he were a stranger, as if he were someone with whom she had no connection. 'What are you suggesting? What possible harm could come to me?'

'It is not a question of harm, Mary.'

'Of what then? Propriety? Custom? Do you think so little of me that you would impose *conditions* upon me?'

'I know Ireland is honourable –'

'But you do not know your sister. When you see me in this house I am sleep-walking. I have no real – no genuine – life here at all. Why do you think I long for you to come home each evening? When you are not wretchedly drunk, of course.' Charles said nothing. 'Whom do I see? Whom do I talk to? Whose propriety is it that I should be pressed to death? Whose convention is it that I am already lying in the family grave?'

'Hush, Mary. You will wake them.'

She raised her voice even higher. 'They will *never* be woken! I am dying here.'

He took her arm and hurried her upstairs into his room. 'Do you want the world to hear you, Mary?'

She sat upon his bed, exhausted. 'Mr Ireland read to me

his latest discovery. I listened. That is all. Then he escorted me back. We parted at the door. As you say, he is an honourable man. I promised him one thing.'

'And what was that?'

'I promised him that you would ensure his essay is published.'

'I really do not understand one word of this. What essay?' His sister's obvious anger and distress had bewildered him. He thought it best, in the circumstances, to remain neutral and indifferent. 'Begin again, dear. What does Ireland want?'

'*Mr* Ireland has discovered a short poem by Shakespeare. It is no more than six or seven lines long. As I told you, he read it to me tonight. But it is the first new verse to be discovered in two hundred years. It is remarkable. Beautiful.'

'I have read the father's essay in the *Gentleman's Magazine*. He mentions only an unknown benefactor. Has his son told you anything more?'

'Nothing whatsover.' She lied easily to him.

'There can be no mistake about it?'

'None.'

He was surprised by her sudden firmness and steadiness of tone. He hoped to encourage it. 'What is it that Mr Ireland wishes me to do?'

'It is a great discovery and, naturally enough, he would like to be the one who divulges it to the world. If he writes an eassy, will you place it for him?'

In truth Charles Lamb did not wish in any way to be associated with William Ireland. He was a tradesman, a shop assistant, who had made a fortunate discovery. It did not confer on him any powers of composition or invention. 'Are you sure, dear, that this is the wisest course?'

'What is the alternative? This discovery is remarkable – astonishing –'

'Exactly so. It must be properly described and documented.'

'I see. You do not think Mr Ireland capable of any proper style.'

'I cannot tell, of course, but is it likely? Is it even possible? He has had no education, by his own account. He was raised entirely by his father.'

'Did Shakespeare have any proper education? I am surprised at you, Charles.'

'He is no Shakespeare.'

'I suppose that only you have the skill to compose literary paragraphs. You think a great deal of yourself, Charles.' Mary's anger seemed to have returned. She bit her under-lip and turned away from him.

He was wary of her now. He had never before witnessed these sudden changes of mood. It was best to placate her. 'Forgive me, dear. It is late. He is no Shakespeare, but he may prove to be another Lamb. I will assist him in any way possible.'

'Can he visit us, Charles, and explain what he intends to write? I would be so glad.'

'Of course. Let him come at his own convenience.'

A short note from Mary to William brought him to Laystall Street on the following Sunday morning. He seemed nervous in Charles's company, and he looked to Mary for reassurance as he read out the Shakespearian verses.

'They are very elegant,' Charles said.

'Exactly so. Elegant.' He seized upon the word. 'Can I read you, Mr Lamb, what I have started to write?' They were sitting in the drawing-room, and Mary noticed the myriad particles of dust floating and spinning in the rays of the spring sunshine. William took from his pocket a sheaf of papers. 'I have neglected the opening. May I plunge *in medias res?*'

'By all means.'

So William Ireland began to read. ' "Another excellence of Shakespeare, one in which no other writer equalled him, lay in the language of nature. So correct was it that we can see ourselves in all he wrote; his style and manner have also the felicity, that not a sentence can be read without its being discovered to be Shakespearian." '

Charles Lamb listened with attention, and was indeed surprised by Ireland's vigour. The young man described the nature of the poem he had discovered, discussed its analogies with known and recognised passages from the rest of Shakespeare's poetry, and then concluded with a flourish. ' "We shall then, after allowing to Shakespeare all the higher qualities that demand our admiration, be compelled from this example to concede to him Milton's title of 'our sweetest bard'." '

Mary clapped her hands together.

Charles had expected the awkward language of the novice, but instead he had listened to an accomplished piece of writing. 'I am very impressed,' he said. 'I hardly —'

'Believed me capable of it?'

'I am not so sure of that. But it is very fluent.'

'Nonsense, Charles. At William's age, Milton was already writing odes.'

'Oh, I have written odes!' Ireland checked himself. 'I owe it in part to you, Mr Lamb. I admire your essays in *Westminster Words*. I would not dare to say that I have caught your style but I was inspired by them.'

'That is a great compliment, Charles. Thank William for it.'

Charles held out his hand, and William grasped it with a friendly flourish. 'So do you think, sir, that it can be submitted?'

'Of course. And I am sure that it will be accepted by Mr Law. May the poem be quoted in full?'

'There would be no point otherwise.'

Mary sat down beside Charles upon the divan, and put her arm round him. 'This is a sunny day in all our lives,' she said.

Her use of the odd phrase prompted Charles to look at her. Her expression was serene, rapt almost, and she was gazing at William with peculiar fervour.

It was this image that he contemplated in the Billiter Inn, in the company of Tom Coates and Benjamin Milton. He was now more than ever concerned for Mary's health, since in the last few days she had developed a cough that left her weak and out of breath. She had become fevered, too – her eyes bright, her face hot and dry. He explained it to himself as the impending change of season.

Three jars of 'Stingo' had been laid before them.

'What ho, Watteau!' Tom Coates raised his jar, and chinked it against that of Benjamin Milton.

'Your very best, gentlemen.' Charles raised his own jar. 'Now tell me this. How are we to while away the lagging time?'

'We can talk.'

'No. Not here. Not now. I am referring to the idle months of summer. The dog days. The days of wine and roses, as Horace puts it.'

'You have it. Drink wine and eat roses. Breathe forth the perfumed breath of Araby.'

'We could hire a balloon.'

'We could make Wedgwood plates.' Tom and Benjamin were determined to outdo one another.

'We could fart inflammable gas.'

'We could play with puppets.'

'We scarcely need puppets.' Charles glimpsed the outline of a scheme. 'Do you recall last year, when the Internal Bond Office performed *Every Man In His Humour*? It was a great success. They charged at the door.'

'And drank the proceeds. The money turned into liquor.'

'No. The money went to the City Orphans. I remember the letter sent to them by Sir Alfred Lunn.' He took a large draught of 'Stingo'. 'This is my plan. We will put on theatricals.'

'Whatever gave you that idea?' Tom Coates was incredulous.

'God.'

'Charles, I cannot walk on stage with a wig and a false beard. It is simply not possible.' Benjamin Milton smoothed back his hair. 'I would look ridiculous. Besides, I cannot act.'

'That is a problem, Ben, I grant you.' Charles was still elated by his conception. 'But, you know, we could use it to our advantage.'

'How so?'

'The answer is coming to me. Wait a little.' He gazed at the ceiling, as if expecting some small fairy to appear on the edge of its moulding. 'Well, I have it. Why did I not think of this before?'

'When have you ever thought of anything before?'

'Pyramus and Thisbe. And the wall.'

'Explain, dearest.'

'The mechanicals in *A Midsummer Night's Dream*. Quince. Bottom.' He looked at Benjamin. 'You will make a very good Snout. The mechanicals are the essence of bad acting. We will perform their play. It will be fantastical.'

'This is certainly a fantasy.' Benjamin was rubbing his nose. 'No doubt about that.'

'Don't you see the mirth of it?' Charles was enamoured of amateur theatricals. He often attended the penny-gaffs and the dramas played in the houses of friends; in the past he had taken on the roles of Volpone and of Bluebeard.

'I see the fun in it,' Tom replied. 'But how can we execute it? We cannot act.'

'Haven't you been listening?' Charles asked him.

'Probably not.'

'This is the point, dear Tom. Neither could Quince or Bottom.'

'But they are characters. We are real. Aren't we?'

'What does it signify, Ben? The words are the same, are they not? We can call in Siegfried and Selwyn.' Siegfried Drinkwater and Selwyn Onions were also clerks in the Dividend Office. 'They would be perfect Athenians. We can perform it in the Transaction Hall. On midsummer night, don't you think?'

Tom Coates and Benjamin Milton looked at each other solemnly, and then burst out laughing.

Chapter Seven

On the stroke of noon William Ireland walked into Paternoster Row; he knew that this was the hour when that week's issues of *Westminster Words* would be presented to the bookshops and booksellers of the street. They were bound up in brown paper and string, and delivered by the editor himself from the depths of a hired cabriolet. William had witnessed this the week before, and the week before that, as he waited impatiently to see if his article on Shakespeare's lost poem had been published. He knew the bookshops of the neighbourhood very well and, as soon as the cab had passed, he asked for a copy of the periodical from Mr Love of Love Volumes.

'A slow time for the trade, Mr Ireland, don't you agree?'

'Every time is a slow time, Mr Love.'

'Well. Never mind it.' He was a gaunt man, with white and wispy hair, who had a habit of looking sideways at anyone to whom he talked. 'This weather is too warm for me, Mr Ireland. They don't like it neither.' He gestured towards his books. 'They like it mild. Well. Never mind it. How's your father?'

William bought *Westminster Words*, and hurried down the Row. He was looking for a secluded spot where he might inspect his copy. He ducked behind a pile of barrels, carefully arranged in a pyramid by the drayman, and opened the periodical. It was the first essay. 'An Unknown Poem by William Shakespeare' was set up in 12 point roman type, and was followed 'By W. H. Ireland'. It was his own name in print. He had never before seen it in that guise and it seemed strangely remote, as if he had always harboured some secret identity that had only now been revealed. He read the first words, so much more serene and significant in this typeface, as if he were reading them for the first time. It was a moment that he had often anticipated, and so it came to him with a sharper pleasure.

It has been concluded heretofore that no further example of William Shakespeare's writing would ever be discovered, and that nothing more would be added to the store of dramatic poetry known to the world. In this, as in so many other matters Shakespearian, the common opinion has proved to be mistaken . . .

Edmond Malone was reading this in a compartment of Parker's Coffee-House off Chancery Lane; he leant back against the oak panels with an expression of surprise, took off his spectacles, and immediately called for his reckoning. He put on his hat and, with *Westminster Words* tucked neatly under his arm, he walked briskly into the street. Within a few minutes he had reached Ireland's bookshop. The bell upon the door alerted Samuel Ireland himself, who had been on his knees beneath the counter examining the faeces of a mouse.

'Good afternoon to you, Mr Malone. Is it the afternoon?'

'It is. What does this mean?' He laid down a copy of the periodical upon the counter.

Samuel Ireland opened it and peered at the first article. He picked it up and held it close to his face, reading it carefully as his breath became shorter and more laboured. 'I have not the least conception —' He took out his handkerchief and blew his nose very loudly. 'I was not told —' He blew his nose again. 'This is a wholly unwelcome surprise.'

'Well, sir, where is it?'

'It?'

'The poem that your son has so lavishly described. The manuscript. I must see it, Mr Ireland.'

'I have not the least idea where it may be, Mr Malone. William has not seen fit —' His anger was growing as he spoke. 'My son has not had the courtesy to tell me anything of this. He has deliberately concealed it from me. He has played false.'

'This poem does not belong to your son. It belongs to the world.'

'I know it, Mr Malone.'

At this moment William Ireland walked into the bookshop. He was still elated by the sight of his name in *Westminster Words*, and greeted their hostile expressions with equanimity. He saw the periodical on the counter. 'You have read it, Father?'

'What is the meaning of it?'

'If you have read it, then you must know. Good afternoon, Mr Malone.'

'I ask you again, what is the meaning of it?'

'I will tell you the meaning. I have done what you told me I never could do. I have written an essay. And it has been published.'

'How could you conceal such a thing from me?'

'You would have taken it, Father. You would have assumed that I had no great skill in composition. Now I have proved you to be wrong. That is all.'

Samuel Ireland glared at his son, but said nothing.

Edmond Malone had, in the meanwhile, become impatient. 'This has nothing to do with father or with son. Where is the poem?' He turned to William. 'It was very rash and hasty of you, sir, to leap into print before you were sure of your ground. How do you know it to be genuine?'

'I am sure of its provenance.'

'Oh yes? Authenticity is proved on instinct, I suppose. Scholars have no place in this court.'

'The beggar is becoming proud,' his father said.

William looked at both of them, and smiled. 'Wait a moment, Mr Malone, if you will.' He rushed upstairs and a few moments later came back with a large envelope. 'I resign this to your care and custody, Mr Malone. Subject it to whatever scrutiny you wish. If you have any doubt that it is Shakespeare's, proclaim that doubt from the rooftops.'

Malone took the envelope eagerly, and extracted the manuscript. 'You state in your essay, sir, that these are love rhymes.'

'Read for yourself.'

'I have had that pleasure. In *Westminster Words.*' Yet he read it over again. 'I am glad to find no indelicacies here. It had been my fear –'

'Indelicacies?'

'Shakespeare was steeped in bawdy. We live in dread that something will be found out. So much ribaldry defaces his poetry.'

'This is very pure, I assure you. I must have your word, Mr Malone, that you will return it within the month.'

'It will be back in your possession sooner than that, Mr Ireland. On my word of honour it will not be harmed or damaged in any way.'

'We must make out a receipt.' Samuel Ireland was suddenly in motion, searching behind the counter for ink and paper.

'My father is of a nervous disposition, you see, in matters of this kind.'

'It is a precious thing, William. It is not a trifle.'

The short declaration was duly signed, and Edmond Malone left Holborn Passage clutching the envelope to his chest.

Samuel Ireland came back from the door, having waved a farewell. 'You should not have given him the document, William.'

'Why ever not?'

'Consider its value. You might as well have given him a bag of guineas.'

'Mr Malone is honourable, is he not?'

'Honour can be bought and sold.' He seemed to regret what he had said. He picked up the copy of *Westminster Words*, and without saying anything read his son's essay. After he had finished it, he handed it to William. 'Why did you not inform me of this poem? Why did I have to read of it in a journal?'

'I have told you why. It was my wish.'

'Your *wish*? Do you acknowledge no duty towards your own father?'

'Of course. As far as nature allows. You informed me that I could not write. You told me, in so many words, that I was fit only to be a shop assistant.'

'That was not what I meant at all –'

'Tell me this, Father. Do you not owe a duty to your son? You might have encouraged me.'

'This is not the time –'

'There never has been a time. You might have nurtured in me some appetite for learning. Instead I have had to educate myself.'

'Just as I did. The best education –'

'– is self-administered. I have heard you say that often. Well. You have read the article. Consider if I have not educated myself properly.'

They continued the argument upstairs, after supper. Rosa Ponting had left the room, professing no interest in the subject of 'them dratted papers', but in fact she put her ear to the door after she had closed it. She could hear Samuel Ireland chinking his glass against his plate in evident annoyance. 'Mr Malone has no rights in this matter. These papers are jewels. You cannot hand them to anyone you please.'

'Is that why you claim them for yourself? Is that why you hawk them around like so many articles for pawn? I found them. I own them. They have nothing whatever to do with Samuel Ireland.'

'That is not fair, William. That is not just. If you were not known to work in my establishment, your patron would not have given you a second glance.'

'That is not so.'

'Let me finish. You are known to the world as my son. My reputation, as much as yours, is at the stake.'

'Well, then, quit yourself of any responsibility. Sign a document denying any interest in the matter. I am sure that Rosa will willingly witness any disclaimer.'

'Why are you saying this to me? The ties that bind a father and a son are sacred.'

'What is mine is yours?'

'That has nothing to do with it. That is low.' Samuel Ireland rose from the table, breathing heavily. 'You may need my help. My advice. Who knows what else you may discover.'

'Such as a love-letter to Anne Hathaway?'

'I beg your pardon?' He sat down again quickly.

'Not a letter, precisely. But a note. A billet-doux. I could not allow Mr Malone to take everything.'

Samuel Ireland laughed out loud. 'Admirable, William. You have the advantage of me. Bring it out. Let me see it.'

William took it from his leather pocket-book. It was a slip of paper, to which a lock of hair had been tied with a thin thread. He had protected the object with a wrapping of fine tissue-cloth and, when he placed it on the dining-table, his father carefully unwound it.

Samuel Ireland was able to read the inscription on the paper. '*I do assure thee no rude hand hath knotted this. Thy Will alone hath done the work. He hath a way. Neither the gilded bauble* – something – something. Excuse me. I am overcome.' The hair itself was of a reddish tinge, curling at one end. He was afraid to touch it. 'Is that,' he asked, 'the genuine thing? *The* hair?'

'Why should it not be? The hair of Edward the Fourth, when he was taken from the grave, was still strong and highly coloured. He died in 1483.'

'Was this found among the other papers? In the house of your benefactor?'

'Of course. Where else? That house will one day become a shrine to all true lovers of Shakespeare.'

'*If* anyone can find it.' On the mention of a love-letter, Rosa Ponting had come back into the room. 'Lord, William, you make such a mystery of everything. It is aggravating. Truly it is. Will you still not tell your father where this person lives?'

'Shall I tell you, Rosa, how she put it to me?'

'Go on. I like a story.'

'She does not think it fit to subject herself to the impertinent questions of any individual. Her husband is lately dead, and left no explanation concerning the papers he collected. She has no more to say and, as a gentlewoman, she does not wish to go before the public.'

Rosa sniffed, and began to clear away the plates.

Samuel Ireland refilled his glass. 'That is very proper of her, I am sure,' he said. 'But there will be questions.'

'Which I shall answer.'

'Her husband must have been a most remarkable collector.'

'Certainly. No snapper-up of unconsidered trifles. I am close, Father, to coming to a conclusion about that. There is no mention of books or papers in Shakespeare's will.'

'I know it.'

'We can assume that his effects were left to his daughter, Susannah, together with his house and land.'

'She married Doctor Hall.'

'Precisely. They in turn bequeathed everything to their only child, Elizabeth, who was still living in Stratford.'

Rosa Ponting came back into the room. 'You will tell us where *her* house is, I suppose.'

'That house was taken over by Cromwell's soldiers during

the parliamentary wars. We know that. The papers are never mentioned again.'

'So you believe that the soldiers took them? Or used them for lighting their blunderbusses?'

'Not exactly, no. There were antiquaries among the parliamentarians. Once one of them learned that the soldiers had occupied Shakespeare's old house, it was easy. A word with the commander of the local forces and then —'

'He is granted access. Who could possibly care what happened to the scribblings of a dramatist? One of the devil's party?'

'Quite so, Father. But they are preserved. They are a private treasure, not to be vouchsafed to the world. They are passed down. And then they are tracked down by my patron's husband.'

'What finer purchase could there be? I wonder how much?' Samuel Ireland went to the small window overlooking Holborn Passage, and gazed down upon the cobbles.

Rosa Ponting was comfortable in an armchair, surveying her needlework. 'Well, Sammy, you told me they can only rise in value. Nice for some.'

Within a week Edmond Malone had returned the Shakespearian fragment; he pronounced it to be genuine, beyond any possibility of serious doubt, and made a point of presenting it to William rather than to Samuel Ireland. 'I must congratulate you, sir, on your assiduity. We are all indebted.'

'And the verse itself?'

'It embodies the sublime genius of the poet. Shakespeare sometimes mingles his effects. It is said that too much farce is mixed with his tragical matter. He puts fools by gravesides and mingles kings with clowns.'

'Is there a difference?'

Malone ignored the question. 'But this is purity itself.'

William's delight was evident; he shook Malone's hand, and then rushed upstairs saying, 'I have something else for you to consider.' He brought back with him the short love-letter and the lock of hair. 'Touch the hair, Mr Malone.'

The scholar would not. He put up his hands, as if in self-defence. He had quickly read the inscription, and understood its significance. 'It is too close to him. In my imagination it is warm and palpable.'

'It would be tantamount to touching him?'

'Indeed.'

William seemed to be amused by this. 'I have shown the lock to an antique wig-maker, Mr Malone, who assures me that it is genuine. It is the hair of the period. Somewhat coarser than our own.'

'I do not doubt it. Nothing surprises me now. It is like some sea of joy.'

'And there is something else.' Samuel Ireland ducked beneath the counter, and came out with a sheaf of papers. 'A complete manuscript.' The sheets had been folded into four parts, and were tied together by some kind of silk thread. The writing was clearly visible. 'It is *Lear*.' He intoned the word as if he were announcing it upon a stage. 'It is not a scribal copy. It is in the original hand.'

'I have examined it with the text,' William said. 'And this is the astonishing thing. It is exact in every particular to the Folio, except that the oaths and blasphemies have been removed.'

His father took up the theme. 'The bard, sir, has silently removed those indelicacies you described to us.'

'I suspect,' William added, 'that this was Shakespeare's copy for the Master of the Revels. He wished to be free of the Master's censorious pen.'

'Very like. That was often the way. The offending lines would then be reinstated in performance.' Malone examined the handwriting very carefully. 'So this is the bard without the blemish of bawdy. It proves without a doubt that he was a much more finished writer than ever before imagined.'

'I trust so,' William replied. 'I believe so.'

'I am holding the papers upon which Shakespeare laboured. It is scarcely credible.'

'Yet it is so, Mr Malone.'

'I never thought, in my lifetime –' He broke off, and suddenly burst into a fit of weeping. William helped him to a chair, where he mopped his eyes with a handkerchief. 'I apologise. Excuse me.'

'No need for any apology in the world, sir.' Samuel Ireland was beaming at him. 'We have all done it. It is a natural response. It is inevitable. I have wept many times.' He looked at William, and smiled. 'I have not been able to contain my feelings. My son is made of sterner stuff, I believe.'

'No, Father, you are mistaken. I could have cried for joy at any time in these last few months. It is overwhelming.'

'That is the word.' Malone rose from the chair. 'Overwhelming. It allows me to ask you once again. Where do these treasures come from?'

'It is not in my power.'

'I must repeat myself. Can you tell us the source of these papers? The origin?'

'And I can only repeat to you what I have told my father. My benefactor does not wish to be known or named to the public, since it would provoke excessive interest and speculation in one who wishes to remain retired from the world.'

'This personage,' Samuel Ireland added, 'has our entire loyalty and trust.' William looked at his father in surprise. 'He has asked for the utmost discretion, and he has been pledged it. It is a sacred honour, sir, with which we are rewarded by these gifts.'

'I regret it very much. But the polite world will no doubt applaud your sentiments.' Malone seemed about to leave, but then hesitated. 'Talking of the world, Mr Ireland, I have a proposal. It is not enough to read of these Shakespearian items. They should be seen. They should be displayed.'

'I am a little ahead of you, sir. My son and I have decided that they will be shown here.' Again William looked at his father in astonishment. 'These humble premises will become a Shakespearian shrine. Was not that your word, William?'

'I cannot think of many words at the moment, Father.'

'A shrine to the bard.'

'I am glad of it. I am delighted.' Malone wiped the last tears from his face. 'You must place an advertisement in the *Morning Chronicle*. We all read it. May I send, Mr Ireland, one or two idolaters to the shrine? Before it is advertised?'

'Of course, sir. Only too happy.'

When Edmond Malone had gone William turned to his father. 'What was that about my patron? A *gentleman*? You are digging yourself too deep, Father.'

'It pleases Mr Malone to believe that he has our trust.'

'I do not give a damn what pleases Mr Malone.' William banged his fist against a low shelf. 'And what do you mean? A *shrine*?'

'I did not tell you for fear of *ruining the surprise*.' William did not realise that his own words were being quoted back at him. 'Do you not see? The interest will become so great that we will have countless callers.'

'Not if they have no notion where to call.'

'Be serious, William. We must prepare ourselves. We must lay out the evidence where it can be examined at leisure by the various interested parties.'

'Here? In the shop?'

'In the establishment. What better place for it? We have the counter under glass, and the shelves. We can place a sign in the window announcing "The Shakespeare Museum". For a small charge of admission –'

'No! I forbid it!'

'There must be a small fee. Rosa can stand by the door.'

'Absolutely not! No money can change hands. Never!'

Samuel Ireland was surprised by his son's vehemence. 'If that is your wish.'

'It is.'

'Then there is no more to be said.'

'Good.'

'Except this. I am not a wealthy man, William. You know our proceeds. You cannot become rich with books alone.'

'I will not listen to you, Father.'

'If ever there was an opportunity to redeem our fortunes, this offers it. Shakespeare himself was a businessman. He lived from his profits. Do you think that he would condemn us?'

'None of this, Father, is being done for money's sake.'

'Then what was it done for?'

'It was done for *you*.'

'I confess I do not see.'

William laughed, embarrassed by his admission. 'You are like blind Tiresias. Led by a boy.'

'You take the words from my mouth.'

'I am used to that, Father.' William suddenly lowered his head. 'Very well. I have no objection at all to displaying the papers here. If you will agree with me that no payment is involved, I will gladly show them here under supervision.'

His father looked away for moment, his eyes shifting to the middle distance. An increase in numbers might mean a growth in custom; many scholars and literary devotees would come to Holborn Passage for the first time, driven by curiosity or obsession, and would survey the stock of the shop as well as the Shakespearian productions. It was still a worthwhile enterprise. 'Agreed, William,' he said. 'I bow to your superior judgement.'

Yet already, that same afternoon, one of Edmond Malone's particular friends arrived on his recommendation. Thomas Rowlandson, artist and caricaturist, middle-aged and short of breath, entered the bookshop in a flurry of embarrassment and apology. He was wearing a sky-blue jacket with a maroon waistcoat and green plaid trousers. 'This is the place? The soil where Shakespeare has been newly planted? Excuse me. Mr Malone pointed me in this direction. And are you Mr Ireland?'

William held out his hand, but Samuel Ireland stepped forward. 'We both have the honour of that name, sir.'

'I am glad to hear it. Has Mr Malone mentioned me at all? Rowlandson, sir.'

'You are known to all lovers of Shakespeare, sir.' Samuel Ireland was referring to a series of prints that Rowlandson had executed, showing scenes from the plays. It had been published as *The Shakespeare Gallery*.

'Dictated by a higher power. You know who.'

'You honour us, Mr Rowlandson.' Samuel Ireland now shook his hand.

'Simply Tom.'

'You are the first in our museum. But you have caught us unprepared as yet.'

Rowlandson was perspiring very freely. 'Do you have a lemonade? A ginger-beer? Feeling myself rather thirsty, you see.'

'Or something stronger?' William had noticed the signs of weakness on his face. 'Whisky, sir?'

'Just a touch. A drop. In soda water, if you would be so kind. Just the minutest amount.'

William climbed the stairs to the dining-room, and took from a decorated cabinet a crystal decanter of spirit; he poured a large measure, and then from a jug in the adjacent kitchen added a small portion of water. Rowlandson had been waiting for it with some impatience, and only began to speak after he had swallowed it down. 'Malone tells me that you have a letter to Mistress Hathaway.'

'With a portion of the bard's hair.' William took the empty glass from Rowlandson's hand.

'May I?'

'Sir?'

'I simply want to touch the hair.'

'You may.' William fetched the token from a drawer beneath the counter, and presented it to the visitor.

'This is the letter? This is the genuine Shakespearian thing? The hair is like yours, sir. Chestnut turning into flame.' He looked at the young man strangely, almost shyly, but William was already retreating upstairs. He filled the glass with whisky and a little water before returning to the shop, where Samuel Ireland was standing in one of his customary positions – his legs astride, his back very straight, his thumbs in the pockets of his waistcoat. Rowlandson was reading the note to Anne Hathaway. 'This is good,' he said. 'This is exact. Young love.' He read out the sentence that seemed to refer to the specimen of hair itself. '*Neither the gilded bauble that environs the head of majesty, nor honours most weighty, would give me half the joy as did this little work for thee.*' He gave the paper back to William, and eagerly took the proffered drink. 'This is delicious, sir. I am referring to the letter. This is moving. This is the genuine spirit. Again I mean –' He gave out a peal of high laughter. 'The true note is struck in this missive. Just one more, if you please. A little. The tiniest fraction.'

Samuel Ireland was standing in the same position. 'We have another treasure,' he was saying. 'A complete manuscript of *Lear*.'

'In his own hand?'

'We believe so.' William filled his glass again. 'He has changed the indelicacies.'

Rowlandson remembered a line from the play. '*Oh the blessed gods!* Act Two, Scene Two.' He sat down heavily upon a chair.

'Though spoken by Regan, sir.'

Rowlandson looked up at William with admiration. 'You have a sharp mind, Mr Ireland. And you have a charming smile.'

'It is one of the expressions the bard has altered. It has

become, "*Oh you bless'd pow'rs*". Blessed must become a mono-syllable in order to preserve the metre.'

Samuel Ireland brought out the *Lear* document. He presented it to Rowlandson with the suspicion of a bow. And the artist, putting down his drink, rose to his feet. His hands were trembling as he held the pages of the manuscript. 'My forehead, you see, is hot and flushed. Observe it. His fire is heating me.' Then, to William's amazement, Rowlandson went down upon his knees. 'Now I can die contented. I kiss the record of the bard, and give thanks to God that I have lived to see it.'

'Please be seated,' Samuel Ireland urged him. 'You will injure yourself. The floor is very rough.'

William suspected that Rowlandson had been half-drunk when he had first arrived, and he helped him as he rose unsteadily to his feet.

Rowlandson held him tightly by the arm. 'Oh lord,' he muttered. 'The energy and grace of it. You have honoured me, Mr Ireland, with the sight of your jewels.'

'You honour us, sir.' Samuel Ireland was determined not to be overlooked.

'You are an artist, sir,' William said. 'You comprehend.'

'I know it.' Rowlandson continued holding William's arm.

'Then can you tell me this? The bard tells us that the truest poetry is the most feigning —'

'*Love's Labour's Lost*, I believe.'

'Does he mean we will admire what is false?'

'It is a mere conceit of Shakespeare's.' Rowlandson took William's hand in a playful gesture. 'The feigned can never be more true than the real. Chaos would come again.' He sat down heavily in the chair, and drained the last of his drink. 'Besides, it is not a great interest of mine.'

'I only put the question.'

'You must not put questions, Mr Ireland. You must give us answers. Bring forth new papers!'

There were other visitors over the next few weeks and, when Samuel Ireland placed an advertisement in the *Morning Chronicle* concerning 'The Shakespeare Museum', their number increased.

William had discovered some related items – a letter from the Earl of Southampton to Shakespeare, a summons to the dramatist for non-payment of church rates, a short note from Richard Burbage on stage properties – and the bookshop had indeed come to resemble a cabinet of Shakespearian curiosities. William himself had no wish to manage or to supervise the proceedings. That role was reserved for his father, who had purchased a new bottle-green jacket from the firm of Jackson and Son in Great Turnstile Street. Rosa Ponting sat, with her needlework, on a chair by the door. She was there ostensibly to safeguard umbrellas and coats, but it was Samuel Ireland's hope that she would be mistaken for a collector of entrance fees: she did not object to silver being pressed into her hand, and swiftly placed the money in a large work-bag that also contained her fan, her snuff-box, her purse and her handkerchief. She welcomed each visitor in the same fashion. 'The play is in the left-hand cabinet together with the letters. The receipts and bills are on the adjoining counter. Please not to touch the glass nor spit upon the floor.'

She enjoyed her role. As a child she had helped her mother on a fruit stall in Whitefriars Market, and had enthusiastically joined the cacophony of voices that accompanied each day's trading. She had shouted 'Pippins' till she was hoarse. In fact she guarded the bookshop and its exhibits with exemplary care. She knew every tread on the wooden boards; she could tell if someone attempted to climb the stairs, or to wander behind the counter. If a visitor so much as breathed on the glass, she turned her head sharply and glared at the offender. She had no interest in, or curiosity about, Shakespeare as such; but she was pleased that William was advancing the family's fortunes in such an unexpected manner.

That they were a family she had no doubt. She was in fact secretly married to Samuel Ireland. They had been joined, without ceremony, by a naval chaplain in Greenwich; it was only on this condition that she had moved into Holborn Passage. William's mother had died in childbirth and the infant had been taken by the midwife to the midwife's sister in Godalming, in which family he remained until he was three years old. William remembered nothing of this, and his father did not enlighten him. He was returned to Holborn Passage soon after his third birthday, when he was greeted by Rosa with arms outstretched. The small boy had looked away, and cried. He seemed pleased by the surroundings of the shop, however, and, as Rosa put it to her husband, 'took more kindly to the books than to the people'. Rosa was in fact hurt and perplexed by him. He met all her attempts at affection with brusque inattention. She would question him about the small events of the day, as he grew older, but he would reply only very briefly – sometimes with no more than a nod or a shake of the head. He never began a conversation with her and, on the infrequent occasions when they were alone together, he would take up a book or walk over to the window. And, over the years, nothing had changed.

'You might think,' she had said to Samuel Ireland, at the

breakfast table a month after 'The Shakespeare Museum' had opened, '– pass me the damson – you might think that he did not really live here at all.'

'He has immortal longings, Rosa.'

'What does that mean when it's at home?'

'Shakespeare has got into his head. Nothing will ever satisfy him now.'

'Speak sense, Sammy.'

'He does not believe that he belongs here. With us. He is on a higher level.'

'With Mary Lamb, I suppose. You know she has come here twice this week? To see the Shakespeare, or so she says.'

'She is a lady, Rosa.'

'And I am not?'

'She is a young lady.'

'And a very plain one, if you ask my opinion.'

'I know it. But William is not your usual young man. He sees into her soul.'

'I would like to know what spectacles he uses.'

'He has set her apart. He thinks of her as his salvation.'

'From what?'

'From us. Listen. He has come back.'

Samuel heard the lock turn in the bookshop beneath.

Over recent days Samuel had become sensitive to his son's exits and entrances. The morning before, he had left the shop immediately after William. He had watched him turn the corner of Holborn Passage and then swiftly followed. He surmised that he was on his way to the house of his patron, where the Shakespearian papers had been preserved. Samuel was only too eager to track down his son's benefactor and to question her. William was walking south, down one of the narrow lanes that led directly into the Strand; he had a quick, determined step and knew his way among the stalls, the street-traders and the carts that always clustered in the vicinity of Drury Lane. Samuel found it difficult to keep him in view, as he weaved among the itinerant population of the neigh-bourhood, skirting the piles of rubbish and manure, manoeu-vring around the children playing in the street, dodging the baskets and barrels being carried in every direction. Then he caught sight of William crossing the Strand, and took advan-tage of a crush of carriages halted in the road to decrease the distance between them. William entered Essex Street, on the way down to the Thames, but then he turned left and disappeared.

Samuel followed him as quickly as he could; for such a stout man he was surprisingly swift and nimble, partly the conse-quence of many lessons in Russell Square with a French dancing master who had taught him the cotillion and the polonaise. William had walked the length of Devereux Court by the time his father had reached the corner of Essex Street; he peered around the brickwork just as his son pushed open the great wooden door that granted access to the Middle Temple. There was a large open court beyond this door. Could he risk being seen there by his son? He was hardly incon-spicuous. Yet he could not turn back now. It was even possible that the Shakespearian treasures were being hoarded in cham-bers of the Middle Temple itself. He pushed open the door and looked around it. His son was standing by a fountain, his back turned to him, and Samuel scuttled over to an adjacent doorway where he could shelter without being seen. He could hear the spray of water falling into the basin, and the sound of the pigeons gathered around it. He did not wait long for William's presence there to be explained. A woman in a shawl and bonnet passed him, without looking up, and he knew that it was Mary Lamb. So this was their trysting-place.

He looked out from his refuge. They were standing beside the fountain, and William was pointing towards Middle Temple Hall. This was the place where *Twelfth Night* had been performed soon after Shakespeare had written it. They walked around the base of the fountain, talking quietly. Samuel Ireland decided to leave them here. He had seen enough to realise that his son was not about to visit his patron but was engaged in a more private pursuit. Some prompting of delicacy or conscience persuaded him to abandon the chase. He did not wish to watch his son in courtship or dalliance.

Mary and William turned into Pump Court, where they stopped to admire the antique sundial with its stone emblem of 'All Devouring Time'. 'I am sure,' William was saying, 'that Shakespeare had no wish to resemble his father. He loved him, but he did not want to be like him.'

'Of course he did not wish to be a butcher.'

'No. I mean that he fled from failure. A merry failure, but a failure none the less. He hated debt. He hated the pity of others.' They walked through the court, with the Round Church of the Templars by the side of them. 'He was clear-headed. Determined. Full of energy.'

'Ambitious?'

'Of course. How could he have accomplished so much? Look at the gargoyle above that doorway.'

'Charles says that this church is like the background for some pantomime.'

'Your brother is fond of fanciful comparisons. Shall we go in?' They entered the cool space of the circular nave, with the figures of the knights lying upon their backs in a circle around them.

Mary was intrigued by these images of old time. She walked over to each one, in turn, and looked down upon the visages of stone. She found it easy to imagine ancient halls and flickering fires. There would have been smoke, and dogs, and minstrels. When she looked up, William had gone. He was waiting for her in Pump Court. 'It is easy to feel devout in such an atmosphere,' he said. 'But I hate a fugitive and cloistered virtue. These knights belonged in the open air. In the world.'

'I am sure you cannot blame them for lying down.' She realised how little she knew him. 'They must be tired after their adventures.'

They walked out into King's Bench Walk.

'And what will *we* have accomplished?' he asked her. 'How will *we* be remembered?'

'Surely you know by now that your name will be linked with that of Shakespeare?'

He laughed at this. 'Is that enough? Do you think that anyone could be satisfied with that?'

'Very many.'

'You don't understand me as yet, Mary. The papers are merely a beginning. I grant you they were a piece of good fortune. It is a great honour to find – what I have found. But once I have acquired a name, then I must use it. I must prove my worth.'

'Charles predicts a great career for you. He believes you to have a singular talent.'

'For what, exactly?'

'For composition. He admires your essays in *Westminster Words*.'

'One or two merely. Mr Law has asked me to write about Bankside. As it was.'

Although Mary had lived in London all her life, she was unclear about any area beyond her immediate neighbourhood. In this she was not so different from her neighbours themselves. 'I am not sure what you mean,' she said.

'Southwark. South of the river. Over there. Where the Globe once stood. And the Bear Garden. He wishes me to paint a picture of the scene in Tudor times in contrast to the modern. Do you know that, in Shakespeare, modern means ordinary or trivial?'

'May I come with you?'

'Is that not significant, Mary? To be modern is for him to be commonplace. Uninteresting. We think of the Elizabethans as colourful and richly tapestried, but he preferred to look back at Lear and Caesar. What was that you just said?'

'May I come with you to Southwark? I have never been.'

'By all means. It is rough, Mary. And dirty.'

'That does not concern me. It is where Shakespeare lived and acted?'

'So it is said.'

'Then I must see it.'

From King's Bench Walk they went down to the river.

'My father has been watching us,' he said.

'What?'

'I was followed by him.' He laughed, a little uneasily.

'But there is nothing –'

'Nothing between us? I know. But that was not why he

pursued me. He wanted Shakespeare.' Mary did not reply. She was subdued, perhaps, by his open acknowledgement that there was 'nothing' attached to their friendship. 'He wants to track that river to its source. He doesn't trust me.'

'Not trust you? Your own father?'

'He has a strange disposition. Where money is concerned, he becomes fierce.' They walked on in silence for a few moments. 'He wishes to know where the papers are kept. He considers them to be some hoard of gold concealed in a merchant's cave, like something from a fairy story.'

'And you are the prince who holds the lamp.' She found the allusion oddly satisfying. 'You command the genie.'

'Hey presto. And the golden coins are heaped about me. So he follows me, to find the cave.'

'But how can he not trust you?'

'Do you trust me?'

'Of course. I would proclaim your honour here, if you wish. I would swear your truth anywhere!'

'Don't go to the stake for it.' He seemed surprised by her vehemence. 'You might get burned.'

On the side of the walk a young woman with bare feet was playing a violin. Her pale lips seem to move in time to the tune of 'This Blessed Isle'. She had come up from the riverside in search of halfpennies or farthings. The right side of her face was disfigured by some growth or goitre. Mary looked at her with an expression of wonder and then, without the least hesitation, took her purse from her work-bag and laid it at the woman's bare feet.

When she came back, the tears were running down her cheeks. 'It is the absence of love,' she said. They walked a little further, and passed the ruined foundations of the Templar gate. 'But, then, what does that mean to these stones?' She peered at them, as if they were a thousand fathoms deep.

When they turned back the young woman was still playing the violin. As they passed her Mary clutched William's arm, as if she feared some kind of retribution. They walked on into Pump Court and, as soon as they had gone from view, the young woman stopped playing and picked up the purse. Then, very nimbly, she unfixed the goitre from the side of her face and slipped it into her pocket.

Chapter Eight

'*That will ask some tears in the performance of it. If I do it, let the audience look to their eyes. I will move storms.*' Charles Lamb was playing
Bottom in the garden of his house in Laystall Street, with the
rest of the company around him. Tom Coates was Snug and
Benjamin Milton took the part of Quince; they had persuaded
their two colleagues, Siegfried Drinkwater and Selwyn Onions,
to take on Flute and Snout. And they had enlisted Alfred Jowett,
a friend of Siegfried and clerk in the Excise Department, for
the role of Starveling. On this Sunday morning they sat together,
rehearsing their lines, in the small pagoda that Mr Lamb had
set up in the garden ten years before. It had fallen into a state
of some disrepair, its paint flaked and its metal rusting, but it
provided shelter from the light summer shower that was falling
as they delivered the lines under the direction of Mary Lamb.
'Intone, Bottom,' she told her brother. 'Give it depth.'

'*Yet my chief humour is for a tyrant. I could play Hercules rarely, or a part to tear a cat in, to make all split.* Then there comes the verse. Do I need to say it, Mary?'

'Of course, dear.'

Tom Coates and Benjamin Milton were whispering together. When she called her brother 'dear' they were suddenly convulsed with silent laughter. Benjamin put a handkerchief up to his mouth, and seemed to be in agony. Charles ignored them but Mary glared at them before enquiring, very casually, 'What is so funny, gentlemen?'

'Isn't this meant to be a comedy?' Tom could barely speak.

'You make a very good Bottom, dear,' Benjamin whispered before collapsing again in suppressed laughter.

Siegfried Drinkwater was waiting to appear in this scene, and was already growing impatient. 'Could we rehearse Flute now, please? Otherwise I shall forget my lines. I know I shall.'

'They are only short lines,' Alfred Jowett told him. 'They are hardly there at all.'

'I promise you I will forget them, Fred.'

Siegfried Drinkwater was an impulsive young man who dreamed perpetually of the past glories of his family. He announced to the world that he was seventh in line to the throne of Guernsey, and was not at all embarrassed by the fact that such throne no longer existed. His friendship with Alfred Jowett puzzled the others, however, since Jowett was practical, hardheaded and a little mercenary. He divided his salary by the length of the working year, and had calculated that he earned five pence and three farthings every working hour. He had a written table inside his desk and, whenever he managed to idle away one of those hours, he added that sum to his running profit. He and Siegfried would often visit the minor theatres after their day's business was concluded. Siegfried would watch the small stage with unaffected delight, and would frequently shed tears at some unfortunate turn in the drama, while Alfred would stare placidly at the actresses and the female 'extras'.

'I cannot see the point of doing this comedy,' Mary said, 'if there is to be giggling all the time.'

'In Barrow's sermons,' Selwyn Onions told her, 'giggling is known as wagging the lungs. It is called a hum.'

This was too much for Tom Coates, who bent double in his chair. Selwyn was well known for his helpful explanations. Yet he was also known for being almost always wrong, in matters of fact and detail. 'Selwyn says . . .' had become a phrase in East India House, implying that complete nonsense was about to be uttered.

They had reached that part of the scene where Siegfried, as Flute, first appears at Peter Quince's call of '*Francis Flute, the bellows-mender?*'

'Am I a bellows-mender? I thought I had something to do with flutes. The name suggests it.'

'No, Siegfried.' Benjamin Milton momentarlly left his part as Quince. 'It has to do with the quality of your voice. It must be flautine.'

'Which is?'

'Light. Reedy.'

'Not tripping or musical?'

'That is not mentioned in the text. Elizabethan flutes were known for their reediness. They were weak.'

'I beg your pardon. No Drinkwater has ever been weak. Ask the people of Guernsey.'

'Just raise it a little higher, Mr Drinkwater.'

'What was that, Miss Lamb?'

'Let your voice ascend a scale. Say the line again, Mr Milton.'

'*Francis Flute, the bellows-mender?*'

'*Here, Peter Quince.*'

'*Flute, you must take Thisbe on you.*'

'*What is Thisbe, a wandering knight?*'

'*It is the lady that Pyramus must love.*'

'*Nay, faith, let me not play a woman.* I will not play a female.' Siegfried was very indignant. 'You told me, Charles, I played an honest workman.'

'And so you do.'

'I will not put on a dress.'

Selwyn Onions was once more ready to intervene. 'You need only wear a smock or pinafore.'

'I beg your pardon? Did I hear you correctly? A *pinafore*? That is not a word a Drinkwater knows.'

Benjamin Milton and Tom Coates were listening to this conversation with undisguised pleasure. Benjamin took out a hip-flask of porter, and managed a surreptitious draught. He handed it to Tom, who turned his back to drink from it. Alfred Jowett leaned over to them. 'What a thing to be doing on a Sunday morning. Are they at church?' He gestured towards the Lambs' house.

'I don't believe so,' Tom said. 'But Mrs Lamb is a devout person. Or so I am told.'

'I hear that Daddy is a hatter.'

'What?'

'As mad as.' He put his finger up to his head. 'It runs in the family.'

Mary Lamb was repeating the next line for Siegfried. '*Nay, faith, let me not play a woman: I have a beard coming.* You see that you *are* a man, Mr Drinkwater. There is no doubt about it.'

'Will the audience know it?'

'Of course. We will give you a tall hat. There will be no mistaking your sex.'

Mary had splendid visions of this play. When Charles had asked her to prompt and direct his colleagues, she had been delighted. Over the last few weeks she had sensed a superfluity of energy within herself, a barely repressed excitement, and she wished to divert it. So she seized eagerly upon this short comedy, concerning the mechanicals, within the larger comedy of *A Midsummer Night's Dream*. She had helped Charles to connect the separate scenes, and had even furnished some additional dialogue and stage business for the purposes of continuity. She had said nothing to William Ireland, however, about the enterprise. She was sure that he would have felt excluded. She was also sure that he would have arrived at the wrong conclusions. It was one of those complicated human situations that Shakespeare was able to explain so clearly. William Ireland would have deemed himself rejected because he was a shopkeeper. The fact that he had literary aspirations would only have compounded the insult. He was a parvenu, not fit to mix with gentlemen. In fact his trade had nothing whatever to do with it.

'Shall we invite Mr Ireland to act with us?' Charles had asked his sister.

'William? Oh no.' She answered quickly. 'He is too –' The word 'sensitive' had occurred to her. 'Too serious.'

'I know what you mean. He would not appreciate our little diversion.'

'Shakespeare has become a holy cause with him.'

'He would know our intentions are good.'

'Of course. But William is devoting so much time and attention to the papers –'

'He cannot see the light side of it.'

'Not yet. Not now. Reserve that for your friends.'

Charles Lamb already suspected that his sister was more attentive to William Ireland than she cared to admit. Her solicitousness, her tremulous regard for what she perceived to be his feelings, confirmed her interest. He had the sudden image of a stricken deer; whether it was William, or Mary, he could not say.

'*Have you the lion's part ready?*' Tom Coates was reading the part of Snug. '*Pray you, if it be, give it me; for I am slow of study.*'

'And that's true, too.'

'Mr Jowett, please not to interpose. Go on to your line, Mr Milton.'

'*You may do it extempore, Snug, for it is nothing but roaring.*'

'Do you think, Mr Milton, that you could sound a little more common?' Mary was intent upon the text, and did not look up. 'Could you be coarsely spoken?'

'That will be extremely difficult, Miss Lamb.'

'Do, please. He cannot be a clerk. He must be a carpenter.'

Charles had noticed with some surprise how intently and eagerly his sister had guided their proceedings. It seemed to him now that she did everything to the extreme. In recent weeks also she had been nervous and ill at ease. She had been peremptory, in particular, with her mother.

Three days before, Mrs Lamb had scolded Tizzy for bringing in burnt toast. 'Whatever is the matter with you?' she asked the old servant. 'Mr Lamb cannot abide a hard crust.'

Mary flung a teaspoonful of sugar, which she had been holding above her cup, on to the table-cloth. 'This is not a house of correction, Mother. We are not your prisoners.'

Mr Lamb looked at her, half tenderly and half admiringly, and whispered, 'Left at the landing. Last door.'

Mrs Lamb said nothing, but looked in astonishment as Mary rose from her place and left the room. Charles was buttering the toast with all the signs of thoughtfulness. 'I do not understand that girl,' she said. 'She is so changeable. What is your opinion, Mr Lamb?'

'North by north-east,' he murmured, to the apparent satisfaction of his wife.

Charles was inclined to ascribe Mary's erratic behaviour to her friendship with William Ireland; the young man was making her restless. He did not blame him particularly for this; so far as he could tell, his conduct was exemplary. But Mary had never before entered any relationship of trust with a comparative stranger. It was as simple, and as serious, as that.

<hr>

"*Cos it ain't nuffink but roarin*'.' Benjamin Milton was now playing the part of Quince with a broad Cockney accent.

'Well done, Mr Milton. But do you think a rustic dialect might be more suitable?'

'Something rural, Miss Lamb? Do you have any model in mind?'

'Have you heard the lectures of Professor Porson on classical antiquity?'

'Of course. In the Masonic Hall.'

'Can you conform your voice to his, do you think?'

Tizzy came into the garden, announcing that 'the young man' was asking for Miss Mary at the front door.

'*The* young man?' Benjamin asked, very jovially. Charles curbed him with a glance as Mary, in some confusion, followed Tizzy across the garden through the light summer rain.

She resisted the desire to glance at herself in the mirror as she entered the house. 'You have not left him in the street, Tizzy?'

'Where else can I leave him? Your mother is in the parlour and the hall is full of boots.'

So Mary went to the door and greeted William who was standing, hat in hand, on the top step. 'I am so sorry, Mr Ireland. Forgive me, I –'

'I can't stay, Mary. I was intending to visit Southwark on Wednesday morning.' He hesitated. 'You wished to come with me, if you recall.'

'Of course I remember. I would be very grateful.' This was not the appropriate phrase, and she looked away for a moment. 'I would be delighted. Wednesday morning?' He nodded. 'I will mark it in my diary. Would you care to come in?'

There is a silent communication beneath all words, and William knew that she did not want him to enter the house. He could in any case see Mrs Lamb peering by the curtain, like some castle guard prepared to repulse an attack. 'It is kind of you, but no. I must not. Time is pressing.' He held out his hand, and she took it. 'I will call for you,' he said. 'About nine in the morning?' He left her, hat still in hand, and she watched him as he walked down Laystall Street towards the women congregated around the pump.

She turned back into the house with a sigh, and heard her mother moving quickly to the fireplace. She had no intention of speaking to her, but Mrs Lamb called out in a plaintive voice she knew very well.

'Mary, may I beg a moment?'

'Yes, Ma, what is it?'

'That young man –'

'Mr Ireland.'

'Certainly so. That young man must have beaten a path to this door. He calls continually.'

'What of it, Ma?'

'Nothing. I was merely observing.' Mary remained silent. 'Is it altogether proper, Mary, to play a drama on a Sunday morning?'

'We are not playing. We are reading out some lines.'

'It agitates your father. Just look at him.' He was lying on the divan, watching the movements of a house-fly. Ever since Mary's anger at the tea-table Mrs Lamb had been more circumspect with her daughter; she allowed herself only general remarks and 'observations', or referred to Mr Lamb's feelings on a particular matter. 'He has always kept the Sabbath holy.'

'Then why are you not in chapel?'

'Mr Lamb's feet. They may be mended in time for the evening service.'

Mary was no longer listening. She had sensed a strange dizziness, or lightness, in her head that prompted her to grasp the arm of an easy-chair. It was as if someone had drilled a hole in her skull, and had blown in warm air.

'He never mentions it, but I see him hobbling like a brewer's horse. Don't I, Mr Lamb?' Mary was aware of sound around her, and brushed her face impatiently. 'But he will not complain. Whatever is the matter, Mary?'

Mary knelt down upon the carpet and put her head against the side of the chair.

Her father looked at her, beaming with delight. 'The Lord takes away,' he said.

'Have you dropped something?'

'Yes.' Mary was beginning to recover. She stared at the carpet without seeing it. 'In a minute,' she muttered. 'A pin.'

'I wish I was young enough to bend. Talk of the devil. Charles, help your sister to find her pin. She has mislaid it.'

Charles was surprised to be greeted as the devil as he entered from the garden. 'Where did you leave it, dear?'

Mary shook her head. 'Nowhere.' She clutched her brother's hand, and he helped her to her feet. 'I was mistaken. Nothing is wrong at all.'

'Mr Ireland has just called,' Mrs Lamb said to her son in what she considered to be a significant manner.

'Indeed? Did he not stay?'

'Mary spoke to him at the door.'

'He had other business, Ma.' Mary was leaning on her brother's arm.

'He seems,' Charles said, 'to be a very busy young man.'

In fact Charles was beginning to envy William Ireland. The editor of *Westminster Words* had already published two of Ireland's essays within a month, 'The Humour of *King Lear*' and 'The Word Play of Shakespeare'; he had also invited him to write a series of sketches on 'Shakespearian Characters'. Charles's own essay on chimney sweeps had yet to be published, but Matthew Law had asked him to compose a companion piece on the beggars of the metropolis. The editor had asked him to concentrate upon the more colourful or eccentric of the beggars, rather than the most needy or the most depraved, but Charles had encountered only two or three. There was a dwarf who begged upon the corner of Gray's Inn Lane and Theobald's Road, and who would on occasions dart among the horses in order to scare them. There was a bald-headed woman of St Giles who tumbled in the street for halfpence. But he was not sure that they encouraged any profound reflections upon vagrant life in the city.

Could he consider himself, in any case, to be a writer at all? He was in no sense a professional author; his position at the East India House rendered that impossible. He had no vision to sweep him past all the difficulties and disappointments of the literary life. He contrasted his situation with that of William Ireland, who had found a great theme in his discovery of the Shakespearian papers. Ireland might even write a book.

'Do you wish to continue?' Mary asked him.

'I beg your pardon, dear?'

'In the garden. Have we finished rehearsing?'

'I think so. Yes.' He was governed by Mary's own unspoken desire. She seemed to crave solitude.

'We must all meet again one evening. This week.' She took her hand from Charles's arm, and moved towards the door. 'Ask them to prepare the next scene.'

On the following Wednesday morning Mary Lamb and William Ireland were walking down the steps of Bridewell Wharf towards the water. It had been raining and the wood was worn smooth by continual use. So William took her arm and supported her to the river's edge. She apologised for her slowness. 'This is not very graceful, I'm afraid.'

'It is not ungraceful, Mary. Necessity has its own grace.'

'You say the most surprising things.'

'Do I?' He seemed genuinely curious. 'Ah. Here they are.'

Three or four watermen were standing about the wharf, their boats moored beside them. When William asked to be rowed across they deferred to one Giggs, who had arrived first but who seemed reluctant to leave their convivial conversation. He wore the gilt badge of his trade in his knitted cap, and in an habitual gesture he rubbed it with his sleeve. 'Cost you a tanner,' he said.

'I thought it was threepence.'

'It's the rain. Very bad for the boat.'

'We could have gone across the bridge,' he muttered to Mary as they walked over to the mooring.

'The bridge is so dull, William. This is exhilarating. This is the real thing.'

So they clambered on to the little boat, William taking Mary's hand and guiding her to the wooden seat at the stern. With the ritual cry of 'All right!' Giggs untied the rope and pushed out the boat.

'Will you row us to Paris Stairs?' William called to him.

'That's where I'm going.'

Mary had not been taken across the Thames before, and she lost all sense of herself in these unfamiliar surroundings. 'I feel so small upon the water,' she said.

'It is not its size. It is its past.' The wind seemed stronger upon the river.

'But that does not explain the air, William. It is refreshing. Invigorating.'

'This was the journey he made. When he lived in Shoreditch, he crossed here to the Globe. In just such a boat, too. It has not changed.'

A sloop passed them, going downstream with a cargo of ashes, and the turbulent waters broke against their bows. Mary seemed to enjoy the sensation of being tossed to and fro upon the river. 'I can smell the sea,' she said. 'If only we could turn now and sail towards it!'

Giggs could not hear what she was saying but, observing the delight and excitement on her face, he began to sing one of the water-songs that he had known since childhood.

> 'My sweetheart came from the south
> From the coast of Barbary-a
> And there she met with brave gallants of war,
> By one, by two, by three-a.'

He sang a catch to it, concerning the lowering of a sail, that had some obscene puns on 'cut' and 'slit' and 'hole'. William looked at him in dismay, not daring to admonish him, but Mary could scarcely hide her laughter; she seemed to revel in it, and trailed her hand in the water. 'Here we are in Paris!' Giggs called out before they reached the shore, but they could already savour the powerful scent of caulking tar mingled with fishing-pots and rotten wood. For Mary it was a rare moment of discovery. As they approached the south bank she could see all the life of the river spilling out into the narrow streets behind the sheds and boat-huts along the Thames. They came up to the moorage at Paris Stairs, and Giggs called out 'Oy! Oy! Oy!' to no one in particular. He threw his rope around an iron post, and drew them towards a small wooden landing on to which Mary stepped eagerly. By the time William had paid his sixpence she had already walked into a cobbled lane where the mud flowed freely. 'The bear pit was over there,' he said. 'The audience at the Globe could hear it clearly. It was known as the bear-chant.'

'It is still very noisy here.'

'The people of the river are known for it. It is in their blood.'

'I suppose the water flows in their veins.'

'Very like.'

They walked towards Star Shoe Alley, and he could sense her high spirits. 'More than water,' she said. 'I can smell hops.'

A wind from the south-east had brought the heady aroma of the Anchor Brewery towards them. 'The south is full of smells, Mary. But it has also been a place of pleasure. What greater pleasure is there than beer?'

'Charles would agree with you, I'm afraid.'

'Afraid? There is nothing to be afraid of.' She suddenly noticed that he could barely suppress his excitement. 'There is something I must tell you,' he said.

'What is it?'

'You must repeat it to no one as yet.' He hesitated for a moment. 'I have found it. I have found a new play. It was supposed long lost, but now it has been found.'

'I believe I know what you are saying –'

'Among the papers I have discovered a play by Shakespeare. An entire play. Complete.' They crossed Star Shoe Alley, and passed two women leaning against the doorway of a house with red shutters. William paid no attention to them, but Mary looked back at them in wonder. 'It is *Vortigern*.'

'Was he not a king?'

'A king of ancient Britain. But do you not see it, Mary? This is a new play by Shakespeare. The first in two hundred years. It is a great event. An overwhelming event.'

She stopped suddenly in the street. 'I cannot see around it as yet. I cannot see it properly. Forgive me.'

'It is nothing inferior to *Lear* or to *Macbeth*.' He had stopped beside her. 'Or so I believe. Come. We are attracting attention.' Some ragged children, barefoot upon the cobbles, were advancing towards them with their hands outstretched.

Mary and William walked towards George Terrace, a small row of cottages in an advanced state of dissolution. Some planks had been nailed up in place of windows, and the odour of sewage pervaded the terrace itself.

'I would like you to see it first, Mary. Before anyone else. Even Father does not know of it.'

'I would be frightened of touching it, William, lest –'

'Lest it fell apart in your hands? No need to concern yourself. I have transcribed it.'

'Of course I will read it. But you will not keep it secret for very long?'

'Oh no. It must be published to the world. It must be performed.' William looked in the direction of the river. 'My father is acquainted with Mr Sheridan, so I have hopes of Drury Lane.'

'You have never mentioned Sheridan before.'

'Have I not?' He laughed. 'I assumed that my father had discussed him at length with you. It is his favourite subject.

Now here we are.' They stopped just beyond the row of cottages. 'If Mr Malone's calculations are correct, the original Globe stood just at this point. It formed a polygon. Here was the stage.'

He walked over to a wooden shed that contained white sacks of flour or sugar piled against each other; a boy, with a clay pipe in his mouth, was lounging outside. 'What's it to you?' he asked as William approached him.

'Nothing. I am admiring the area.'

The boy took the pipe out of his mouth, and looked at him suspiciously. 'If I whistle, my pa'll come.'

'No need. No need.' He walked back to Mary. 'This was the yard. The pit where the people stood. Did you know that is the origin of *understanding*? The under-standers were here. They under-stood the action.'

'You have invented that.'

'I have not. It is the truth. And the galleries would have risen all around us. There would have been nuts, and thrushes on spits, and bottled beer. The trumpets sounded three times, to announce the first scene, and then the Prologue entered in black.' He pointed to the boy with the pipe. 'He would have been here. And so would I. We might have watched *Vortigern* together.' His eyes were very bright. 'This whole neighbourhood is charmed beyond reason. Reason cannot explain it, Mary. Do you not see it? The Globe is still here. It still fills this space.'

She looked across the expanse of waste ground, where there were two or three smoke-houses for the preservation and smoking of fish as well as the remains of a dust-heap that had been abandoned by the rag-pickers and the tosh-hunters. 'I am afraid,' she said, 'that the south bank is no longer very glorious. I do not possess your imagination, William.'

'It is not glorious, perhaps —'

'But,' she added quickly, 'it is deeply interesting.'

'As interesting as life, Mary. Is that what you mean?'

'Nothing so grand, I'm afraid. But I like its dust. I like its savour. Nothing here is for the sake of appearance.'

He looked at her quickly. 'Shall we turn back towards the river? You seem tired.'

'Is there nothing else to explore?'

'There is always more to explore. This is London.'

And so they walked east towards Bermondsey, passing the vinegar works and the lying-in hospital on their slow journey through the riverine streets. They turned back at the bridge, after William had warned her that it was not safe to venture further, and took a different route through the cluster of side-streets that had been built over the marshes of Southwark. William suddenly came to a halt. 'Think of it, Mary. A new Shakespeare play! It will change everything.'

'Will it change you?'

'Oh no, I am beyond redemption.'

There was open land beyond, striated with pits and ditches, and they stopped to survey it. Mary turned and looked back at the river. 'What is that in the distance?'

'A water-wheel. It pumps the Thames water through narrow wooden quills. Vortigern is tremendous, Mary. He obtains the throne by murder and by treachery. He murders his mother.'

'He must have been a very wicked man.'

'And then he murders his brother.'

'Somewhat like Macbeth?'

'In essence. But Macbeth never murdered his own family. May I quote a little?'

'May I take your arm for a moment?'

'Of course. Are you faint?'

'Fatigued by the day. You have some lines by heart?'

He supported her arm, and with his free hand gestured into the air as they walked.

> 'O that I could mellow this iron tongue,
> And fashion it to music of soft love!
> But this was my school; thus was I taught,
> And if such tales can please thy tender ear
> Rough and unpolished as most true they are
> Behold the man will sit the live-long day
> Of lingering sieges, marchings, battles, tell
> Where thirsty Mars so glut hath been with blood
> That sick'ning appetite yearn'd out "no more!"'

'It is very striking,' she said. She seemed strangely subdued. 'It has the proper Shakespearian note.'

They had come up to a group of houses just by Paris Stairs. There was the sound of a fierce argument, as between a mother and a daughter, followed by screaming and repeated blows. Mary fled towards the river, and William rushed after her to the water's edge. 'I am sorry you heard that. It is not unexpected here.' He noticed that she was trembling violently. Then she made a movement – it was as if she was falling sideways. And she slipped, or toppled, from the bank into the river below. As she plunged beneath the surface of the water her red dress billowed around her, like a flower suddenly opening into full bloom. William jumped in after her. The Thames was at low tide, and the water by the Southwark side was neither deep nor treacherous. She had gone down some four or five feet before struggling to the surface. William was able to take her in his arms, and steer her towards the wooden landing. His feet had touched bottom, and he propelled her forward with her head above the water. Two watermen, and a fish-wife, put out their arms when they reached the shore and hauled them on to the dry bank. They were both gasping for breath, and Mary vomited water on to the mud and shingle beside the boats. The fish-wife stood behind her and pounded her on the back. 'Get it out, young woman. That's right. The river never yet did good to those who swaller it.'

William was standing upright, but he was surprised by his own weakness. He steadied himself against a mooring post, and stared at the watermen without seeing them very clearly: he still saw, brighter than anything around him, the red dress billowing outward in the shape of a flower. It seemed to him to be the flower of death.

The fish-wife took Mary into a hut, used by the fishermen as storage for their tackle, and William followed. The old woman fired a brazier of charcoal that filled the hut with smoke, but Mary did not cough or choke; she sat with her head bowed, gazing on to the ground.

'You must have slipped upon the wood,' William told her gently. 'It was very treacherous.'

'I'm sorry.'

'There is nothing to apologise for. It could have happened to anyone. To me.'

'No. It was my fault. I should have stopped.'

William did not know what she meant.

'Fine linen dries easy,' the fish-wife said, attempting to comfort her. 'Cotton is hard.' Mary was shivering, and the woman took off her shawl to place around her shoulders. 'You weren't in the river long enough to get sodden. Not like the bodies are.' The she sat down on a wooden crate, opposite William, and began to tell him about the suicides who jumped from the bridge at Blackfriars; a current from the Fleet River, issuing from the opposite bank, in stormy weather sent the bodies tumbling against the wharves at Paris Stairs. 'The eyes, sir, are the worst thing.'

'They will be forced open by the water,' Mary said. 'And the flesh will have acted like a sponge.'

'I know that, Miss.'

William had been drying his jacket against the charcoal fire, but he was still shivering in his wet linen. 'However can they bring themselves to do it?'

'Hardship,' the fish-wife replied.

'You probably think that they are out of their wits,' Mary said to him. 'But the laws of the conventional life do not apply.'

'They are just ordinary mortals, God bless them.' The fish-wife leaned over and touched the edge of Mary's dress. 'They are ill-favoured. But who is not, in this wicked world? The heat is not reaching it, Miss. Go back now before you take any harm. Harry Sanderson will row you.'

Mary stood up and returned the shawl to her. 'I am perfectly well, you see. No fever.'

'Don't speak of fever, Miss. Many have dropped from it here.'

'Shall we take the boat, William?'

They went out to the bank, and the fish-wife called for Harry.

On their return across the river to Bridewell Wharf, Mary began to talk very rapidly. 'Have you by any chance read the novels of Fanny Burney, William? I think not. They would be too low for you. Too feminine. I am surprised you have time for us females at all.'

'I am ashamed to say that I have never read her work.'
William was puzzled by her sudden interest in the subject.
'*Cecilia* is highly recommended.'

'Oh no. Read *Evelina*. The heroine is never understood.
Never properly seen. How could such a young woman come
to terms with the world?'

He was at a loss. 'I will find a copy.'

'I will give you mine! Charles calls it a silly book, but who
cares for his opinions?' She looked across the water to Lambeth.
'What a deal of bother these little boats make on the water!
Do you see them crossing each other's paths? The world is
such a busy place. But it is all unfathomable, don't you think?'

She arrived with William at Laystall Street in a chaise; she
was shaking with cold and exhaustion. Tizzy opened the door
and, startled, stepped back. 'What in heavens has happened
to you, Miss?'

'Don't faint, Tizzy. I am quite well.'

'She slipped,' William said. 'You must unclothe her at once
and put her to bed. Bring her some broth.'

Mrs Lamb appeared in the doorway, in her mob-cap, and
put her hand up to her mouth.

'Restrain yourself, Mother. I am not hurt.'

'Was it the pond?'

'No, Ma, it was the river.' Mary walked into the house,
staggered and fell against the hat-stand.

There was great commotion as Tizzy and Mrs Lamb then
alternately carried and dragged her upstairs to her bedroom.
While William remained nervously in the hall, they undressed
her and laid her beneath the sheets. Tizzy rushed down the

stairs and, without glancing at him, went out into the street. Mr Lamb had caught some sense of the turmoil, because he crept out of the drawing-room and approached William.

'A straw in the wind, is it?'

'Mary is indisposed, sir.'

'Precisely.'

Mrs Lamb now appeared at the top of the stairs. 'Tizzy has gone for the doctor. I must have a few words with you, Mr Ireland. Would you be so good as to heat the kettle?'

'Of course.' He went across to the fireplace in the drawing-room where, even in these days of summer, the kettle could be placed on a metal stand above the coals. He was watching it boil when she hurried into the room.

'Hot gin and peppermint, I think. Otherwise she will contract a fever. How ever did it happen, Mr Ireland?'

'Mary slipped and fell. We were by the Thames at the time.'

'Whatever were you doing by that river?'

'Exploring Southwark.'

'Exploring Southwark?' It might have been located on the Russian steppes.

'In search of Shakespeare.'

'Shakespeare will be the death of her, Mr Ireland. You should not encourage it. Mr Lamb, you should prohibit his books in this house.'

'It was simply an accident –'

'Accident or not, it should never have happened. Where did I put that oil of peppermint?'

She prepared the cordial in a large earthenware bowl, and carried it in stately fashion out of the drawing-room. William turned to see Mr Lamb swigging from the bottle of peppermint. 'Hot,' he said. 'Hot as ice.'

Chapter Nine

Mary had recovered from her fever, having been confined to her bed for two weeks after her immersion in the Thames. In that period she had burned and shivered, calling out for drink and cool air. She had sweated profusely, leading Tizzy to exclaim (much to Mrs Lamb's disapproval) that she didn't know anyone could have so much grease in her, and she had muttered strange words and phrases in her sleep.

William Ireland had visited the house during her illness, but had been told that she was not to be excited or disturbed in any way; the doctor had prescribed sleep and rest. At the end of the second week, however, William had been allowed to talk to her as she sat wrapped in a shawl by the drawing-room window. 'You are better now, I hope?' was his first question.

'It was nothing. A chill. What could I expect?'

'I have brought you something.'

'Is it the play?' He nodded. 'I was half inclined to think it a dream. That day was so strange to me, William. It seems a far-off thing now, and all seems unreal –'

'Yet here it is.' He handed her a bound maroon folder. 'It is real enough.'

She placed it on her lap, and stared out of the window. 'I am almost afraid to touch it. It is a holy thing, isn't it?' He smiled and said nothing. 'It will help me to live.'

'It has been accepted as genuine by Mr Malone. And my father has approached Drury Lane.'

'It will be performed?'

'That is my hope.'

'And yet you know, William, I would have somehow preferred it to remain a secret.'

'Our secret? Oh no. That could not –'

Mrs Lamb came into the room. 'You must rest, Mary. You are not to be excited in any way.'

'I am not excited, Ma.' She looked at William. 'I am exalted.'

'Whatever it is, it is quite enough. We will wish you good morning, Mr Ireland.'

Mary read the play all that afternoon. It was filled with high words and aspiring sentiments, of wonderful cadences and strange magical conjunctions of sound and sense. It was a play of jealousy and mad violence, invoking the ancient British god of vengeance 'whose power turns green Neptune into purple' and who runs 'swifter than wind upon a field of corn'. She believed it to be one of Shakespeare's earliest plays; she compared it to *Titus Andronicus* and the first part of *Henry the Sixth*. Then she read it again, and wondered at the young

Shakespeare's ingenuity. Who else would conjure up the image of a swallow ascending a scene of battle, escaping 'havoc in vast fields below'? Her overwhelming impression was one of gratitude that she was able to read it at all. She was happy to ignore the occasional blemish or ambiguity. She was one of the few who had seen it in these last two hundred years.

She gave the play to Charles that evening, without making any comment. She did not tell him the story of its discovery, in the expectation that he would form his own judgement on its authorship. Charles took it to his room with him after supper, and did not appear again. Just before retiring for the night, she knocked softly on his door.

'Come in, dear.' Charles was at his writing desk, scribbling a letter. 'Is that what you want?' He gestured towards the play, lying upon his bed.

'Have you finished it?'

'Of course. It is not unduly long.'

'And your impressions?'

'Who wrote it? It merely has a title.'

'Could you guess?'

'I refrain from guessing in such matters. It is very like Kyd, but it might be one of the university dramatists. Except that it is not in Latin.'

'No one else?'

'That is a very wide question, dear.'

'It is Shakespeare.'

'No.'

'I can assure you, Charles.'

'It is the most unlike thing to Shakespeare I have ever read.'

'How can you say that? It is quite obvious to me.'

'How so?'

'The majesty.'

'Majesty can be feigned.'

'The periods. The cadences. The diction. Everything.'

He tried to calm her, since she seemed to become anxious. 'It is only a play, Mary.'

'Only? It is the life of the mind!' She stopped a moment, and regained her composure. 'Do you recall Vortigern's words to his wife? *The glass is running now that cannot finish, till one of us expire.* Are they not fine?'

'Fine enough, I grant you.' He got up from the desk and embraced her. 'Dear Mary, this is one of Mr Ireland's discoveries. I knew that at once. But think for a moment. Surely he may be mistaken?'

'Not in so important a subject.'

'How can you be sure? How can *he* be sure?'

'Charles, you are being wilfully blind. Every line breathes of Shakespeare. I could feel him close beside me as I read it.'

'And not someone else?'

'You mean William.'

'You would like to be close to him, too, after all.'

He regretted this as soon as he uttered it. The colour left her face.

'That is unspeakable!' She stepped back from him. 'How dare you!' Then she left the room.

A few days after this conversation between brother and sister, William Ireland was standing before an audience in the Mercers' Hall in Milk Street. He had been invited by the City Shakespearian Society to lecture upon 'The Sources of Shakespeare's Tragedies'. Its president and founder, Matthew

Touchstone, had read two of Ireland's essays in *Westminster Words* and had been impressed by his understanding of Elizabethan idiom. It had been Ireland who had informed him, for example, that 'shadow' was also a term for 'actor'.

William had seemed nervous as he had begun; he had difficulty in enunciating his words, and had taken out a handkerchief to wipe his forehead. He had looked at Mary Lamb, and he had smiled; she was sitting next to her father who nodded vigorously in his direction and raised both hands in the air with immense satisfaction. 'There are other most suggestive sources,' William was saying. 'The celebrated editor and scholar, Mr Malone' – Edmond Malone was also in the audience, having been brought by Samuel Ireland – 'has discovered in the Ancient Indictment Office of Stratford Corporation a most significant document. It is the report of an inquest, held in Stratford-upon-Avon on 11 February 1580. This is the period when the bard is believed to have worked in the office of a Stratford lawyer. Yes, as a young man, he was obliged to earn his living like most others.' He had expected a gentle ripple of laughter but the audience was silent, except for some coughs and the occasional squeaking of boots. 'The document concerns the death of a young woman by the name of Katherine Hamnet or Hamlet.' He had caught their attention, as he knew that he would. 'A death by drowning.' He paused. 'She was unmarried. She had gone down to the River Avon, in which she was later found. It was said by her family that she had walked down to the river in order to fill a pail of water. This is what the inquest concluded.' He glanced quickly at Mary, but her head was bowed. Edmond Malone was sitting in the row behind her, smiling broadly. 'This is how the coroner put it. "*The aforesaid Katherine, standing on the bank of the said river, suddenly and by accident slipped and fell into the same river and there, in the water of that river, was drowned, and not otherwise nor in other fashion came by her death.*" He put down the paper from which he had been reading. 'It is a very emphatic wording, and is clearly designed to forestall the charge of suicide. If Katherine had killed herself, her body would have been denied burial in the churchyard and would have been consigned to unhallowed ground.' Samuel Ireland whispered something to Edmond Malone. 'But there would have been reports of suicide in the small country town. The young Shakespeare, working in the lawyer's office, must have heard them. So there we have it, ladies and gentlemen. A young woman floats upon the river. Her name is Hamlet. Could this be the origin of Ophelia?' William had quite lost his embarrassment, and the anxiety he had felt on beginning this lecture. 'Katherine may have floated down the Avon into immortality.'

Many members of the audience were acquainted with early death; in the conditions of London it was not an unexpected event. In London, too, suicide by water was not uncommon. So they listened quietly, some of them summoning up images of a lost child or relative.

Among the audience was a young man, Thomas de Quincey, who had travelled from Manchester to London a year before. He was thinking of Anne. He only ever knew her as Anne. When he had first come to the city he had known no one; with little money of his own he had appealed to a distant relation, a cousin once or twice removed from his immediate family. This kinsman owned several properties in London, one of them a deserted and broken-down house in Berners

Street; he gave de Quincey the keys, and told him that he might live under its roof until he found lodgings of his own. He accepted the offer gladly, and went at once to Berners Street. He settled himself, with his few possessions, on the ground floor of the house; there was a small piece of rug there, and an old sofa-cover, on which he could sleep. He had a half-guinea remaining for food, and he believed it would suffice until he found employment as a penman or as an office-boy.

On that first night, however, he discovered that he had a companion. The house had one other inmate, a girl of no more than twelve or thirteen years, who had crept there out of the elements. 'I didn't like the wind and the rain,' she told him. 'They are harsh in these streets.' He asked her how she found the house, but she misunderstood his question. 'I don't mind the rats,' she replied. 'But I mind the ghosts.'

She explained how she had come to this situation. It was a familiar London history of want, neglect and hardship that made her seem older than she truly was. They became friends or, rather, allies against the cold and the darkness. They would often walk through the streets together. They went along Berners Street into Oxford Street, stopping at the corner by the goldsmith's, before crossing the road; then they passed the carriage-maker into Wardour Street before turning into Dean Street. Here they always paused at the pastry-merchant. De Quincey had money only for the barest necessities of life, and they stared into the gilt-edged window where an array of pastries, buns and cakes were laid out for sale.

Then de Quincey fell ill with some ague or fever; he managed only what he called 'dog sleep' and spent his days and nights shivering beneath whatever coverings Anne could find for him.

By some miracle of determination, or quick-wittedness, she managed to obtain bowls of hot gruel that she ministered to him. She crept close to him – to 'draw the vapours' from him, as she put it – and dried his forehead with a muslin cloth. After a week of sickness he recovered, and vowed to repay the girl in any way he could.

He was then called away by his cousin, to conduct a small matter of business; de Quincey accepted the commission eagerly, since it would provide him with funds. It obliged him to travel to Winchester, but he promised Anne that he would return within four days. He arrived back in Berners Street five days later, however, and found the house to be empty. He stayed there that night, and for most of the next day, but he remained alone. On the following evening he set out along the familiar streets where as partners in wretchedness they had walked together, but he came back to Berners Street disappointed and disheartened.

He never saw Anne again. She disappeared from the face of London as suddenly and as completely as if she had sunk beneath an ocean. But he mourned for her. He had no notion of what might have happened to her. She was lost. The world itself seemed to breathe misery.

Now he thought once more of her, as William Ireland invoked the spirit of Katherine Hamlet.

William looked up from his notes, and sensed a change in the mood of the audience. He realised, then, what it must have been for Shakespeare to wield power over his auditors. 'I have one other topic of interest to all of us here. An immense topic, if I may put it that way. It concerns the discovery of a new play. Found after two hundred years of oblivion.' He noticed the particular quality of the silence and expectation. Mary raised her head and smiled at him. 'It is entitled *Vortigern*, and dramatises the career of this treacherous and bloody king of Britain. We are reminded of Lear and of Macbeth. It is purely Shakespeare's. The renowned scholar to whom I have already alluded, Mr Malone, has vouched for its authenticity. May I quote his words on this unexpected discovery, of such magnitude to all of us? In Mr Malone's communication to me he states that "this wonderful document is of surpassing interest to all lovers of Shakespeare. Its genuineness is beyond any doubt."' The silence of the audience was then interrupted by sudden and prolonged applause. After a few ritual expressions of thanks, William concluded his lecture.

His father approached him as he left the small writing-desk behind which he had been standing. 'It was magnificent,' he said. 'I could not have given a finer performance myself. You have the magic of the Irelands.'

Malone came up beside them. 'Very fine, Mr Ireland. You have not mistaken eloquence for loquacity, sir.'

Mary was being pushed forward by Mr Lamb. 'Father insists –' she began to say.

'Cabbage and more cabbage!' Mr Lamb shook everyone's hand, including that of his daughter.

'I am delighted to meet you, sir.' Samuel Ireland looked at him with a certain wariness. 'Your daughter is a favourite with us.'

'Have much joy of the worm.'

'Very sage, sir.'

'And gorge at Christmas.'

'I really –'

'We must go, Pa.' Mary took his arm. 'We cannot detain these gentlemen.'

'Ship ahoy!' He beamed at Samuel Ireland but, when he turned to his daughter, he suddenly seemed confused and broken-down.

'This way, Pa. Mind the edge of the carpet.'

'A remarkable old gentleman,' Samuel Ireland said. 'A character.'

Just as Mary was helping her father out of the hall, Thomas de Quincey came up to William. 'May I shake your hand, sir?'

'Of course.'

'The hand that has touched Shakespeare's papers.'

'It was very good of you to come.'

'I have had an interest in Shakespeare ever since I was a child. I grew up in Manchester where, as you may imagine, I was alone in my taste.'

De Quincey seemed eager to talk, but it was not the moment for William to listen. He mentioned to him the address of the bookshop and hurried after Mary, who was vainly trying to hail a carriage at the corner of Milk Street and Cheapside.

'I was delighted to see you and your father, Mary. Thank you for coming.'

'I would not have missed it. And I like to take Father into the world. It cheers him.'

Mr Lamb was staring up at the sky, turning on his heels.

'May I call on you next week?'

'By all means. I long to hear news of the play.'

'You are quite recovered?'

'I am in rude health, William, I am glad to say.'

Three nights previously Charles Lamb had found his sister sitting in the kitchen. She was in her night-dress, and had placed all the cutlery of the household on the table where she was busily arranging it according to length. He had called to her softly, 'Mary, Mary, whatever are you doing?'

She looked in his direction, but stared through him. He recognised at once that she was walking in her sleep. She stood up and went over to the window. She sighed deeply and raised her arms high in the air, muttering, 'Not done yet. Not done yet.' Then she turned and, passing her brother without a sign, went upstairs to her attic room. He put the cutlery back in the drawers, and returned to his own bed.

He had not seen her that next day. She had kept to her room, pleading tiredness. But the following day, Sunday, had been set aside for further rehearsals of the mechanicals from *A Midsummer Night's Dream*. Charles wondered if she would absent herself, but she was at the breakfast table with a copy of the script beside her. 'Tom Coates makes a good Snug,' she said as Charles joined her. 'But I am not sure of Mr Milton as Quince.' She was very brisk.

'He will come round, Mary. He will fill the part. How are you feeling?'

'Feeling?'

'You took to your bed yesterday.'

'I had not slept well. That was all.'

'But you are rested now?'

'Of course. Do you know your lines by heart, Charles? Bottom is very important.'

'Not by heart, dear. By head. Far more satisfactory.'

'It is the same thing.' For some reason she hesitated, before pouring the tea. 'Ma and Pa have gone to chapel. There is no point in waiting for them.'

Over the next hour Tom Coates, Benjamin Milton and the others arrived at the house. They were ushered into the garden immediately by Tizzy, who did not want their 'nasty boots' on her clean floors. It was a bright day, and they sat contentedly enough beneath the decaying pagoda.

'It is all a question of staging,' Benjamin was saying to Tom. 'Snug is portrayed as having a very high voice. And what do you play?'

'The lion.'

'Precisely. Nothing but roaring. Have you ever heard of a lion with a treble roar?'

'And what of Bottom?'

Selwyn Onions could not resist adding a fact. 'He is a weaver, is he not? Did you know that the bottom is the porcelain core the yarn was wound around?'

'So Shakespeare did not mean bottom?' Benjamin was incredulous. 'His nether end?'

'That has nothing to do with it.'

'Ridiculous, Selwyn. What about his line, "*I will move storms*"? That is the cue for a fart if ever there was one.'

Mary came up to them. 'You are all very serious.'

'We have been discussing our parts, Miss Lamb.' Benjamin was a little afraid of Charles's sister.

'Oh, they must be bold. They must be animated.'

'That is just what I have been telling them. They must stride the blast.'

'Well put, Mr Milton. We are about to rehearse the wall scene, gentlemen. Will you take your places?'

Selwyn Onions, playing Snout the tinker, who played the Wall, stood at the back of the garden with his hands wide apart. 'Make sure,' Mary told him, 'that we can see through your fingers. There must be a chink. Charles will be one side of you, and Mr Drinkwater on the other.'

'They are having a tryst, Miss Lamb?'

'Yes. A tryst. Is that not what lovers do?'

'It is a commentary upon the play itself,' Alfred Jowett was telling anyone who would listen. 'It is a play within a play. What is real and what is false? If this is an illusion, is the larger play more true? Or are they both merely dreams?'

Mary was reminded of a recent dream. She had been in a herb garden, savouring the sweet air among the shrubs, when someone had come up to her and said, 'You would be welcome if you were a nun.'

Alfred Jowett was still talking. 'I think Shakespeare knew that his plays were fancies and fictions. He did not confuse them with the true world.'

'He was not trying to impart anything to us, Mr Jowett?'

'No. His purpose was to amuse.'

Charles Lamb and Siegfried Drinkwater, as Pyramus and Thisbe, had taken up their positions on either side of the Wall. Thisbe wrought her voice to a high pitch.

> 'Oh Wall, full often hast thou heard my moans,
> For parting my fair Pyramus and me!
> My cherry lips have often kissed thy stones,
> Thy stones with lime and hair knit up in thee.'

'At the time,' Tom whispered to Benjamin, 'stones was the word for testicles.'

'So Shakespeare is making an obscenity?'

'Of course. I kiss thy balls.'

Charles replied on cue.

> *I see a voice; now will I to the chink,*
> *To spy, and I can hear my Thisbe's face.*
> *Thisbe?'*
> *'My love! Thou are my love, I think?'*

Mary stepped forward. 'Should it not be, Mr Drinkwater, *My love thou art. My love, I think?* She would recognise her lover's voice. And, Charles, you are too restrained for a lover. A lover must breathe passion.'

'How would *she* know?' Benjamin asked Tom in a very low voice.

'Have you not heard? She has an admirer.'

'Mary Lamb?'

'Yes. Charles has told me.'

'That is the strangest news.'

'It hasn't ended yet.'

They returned to the subject a few hours later when, the rehearsals over, they sat in the Salutation and Cat. Charles and the others were standing at the counter; Tom and Benjamin were huddled in a corner, laughing at the events of the morning. 'If Mary Lamb has a lover,' Tom was saying, 'he will need to be careful. She bites. Did you hear her berating Charles for clowning? She was very fierce.'

'It was only in play.'

'I am not so sure. As Bottom, he laughed. As Charles, he winced.'

'What's his name?'

'The admirer is known as William Ireland. According to Charles, he is a bookseller in this neighbourhood.' He paused, to fill his jug from a large bottle of stout he kept beside him. 'He is a great lover of Shakespeare, apparently. He has made discoveries which all the scholars applaud.'

'I kiss his balls.'

'But the question is, does she?'

'*Horribile dictu.*'

Charles was leaning against the counter, listening to a desultory conversation between Siegfried and Selwyn on the subject of the Royal Academy, when he saw William Ireland entering the tavern with an eccentrically dressed young man in a green jacket and green beaver-hat.

Ireland saw him at once, and came over to the counter. The young man in the green jacket stood behind him as he greeted Charles. 'And this,' he said, 'is de Quincey.' The young man took off his hat and bowed. 'De Quincey is a visitor.'

'Where are you staying, sir?'

'I lodge in Berners Street.'

'I have a friend in Berners Street,' Charles said. 'John Hope. Do you know him?'

'London is very large, sir, and very wild. I know no one in that street.'

'But now you know us. Here is Selwyn. And here is Siegfried.' He slapped both of them on the back. 'Over there, in the corner, are Rosencrantz and Guildenstern. How did you meet William?'

'I attended his lecture.'

'Lecture? What lecture?'

'Did Mary not tell you?'

'Not as far as I recall.' With anything concerning his sister, Charles had learned to apply caution.

'I gave a lecture on Shakespeare last week. De Quincey was kind enough to attend. He called on me the following day.'

'And you have become fast friends?' Charles was astonished that Mary had attended this lecture without informing him. 'Will you sit down with me, gentlemen?' He left Selwyn and Siegfried at the counter discussing the suicide of the pugilist, Fred Jackson, and took a table against the wall of the narrow parlour. 'I would like to have heard you,' Charles said.

'Oh. You missed nothing. I am not an actor.'

'Are you not?'

'That is the gift required. To speak with certainty – enthusiasm. I cannot do it.'

'But you have those virtues, William.'

'Easy to have. Difficult to impart.'

Charles did not know whether to mention the play of *Vortigern*: Mary might have lent it to him in confidence. William seemed almost to divine his thoughts. 'How is Mary? She seemed a little tired at the lecture. After her fall –'

'Quite recovered. Blooming.' Charles still could not guess the extent of William's affection for his sister. 'You have given her a new interest.'

'Oh yes?'

'In Shakespeare.'

'She was half in love with him already.'

'My sister is never half in love. She is always at extremes.'

'I understand that.' Ireland turned to his companion. 'Well, de Quincey, you are in good company. Charles is a writer, too.'

De Quincey looked at Charles with interest. 'Have you published?'

'Only small things. Essays in *Westminster Words*. Nothing more.'

'That is a great deal.'

'De Quincey writes essays, too, Charles. But he has yet to find a publisher. He is waiting to be born.'

'I scarcely think about it.' De Quincey blushed, and drank quickly from his glass. 'I hold out no great hopes.'

They drank into the evening, growing louder and more animated by the jugful. The others had gone, but the three of them remained. Charles had informed William of the mechanicals' play, forgetting that Mary had warned him to avoid the subject. He had also told him that he wished to resign from East India House and become a novelist. Or a poet. Anything but what he was.

'I am disgusted,' de Quincey was saying, 'that each of us has such a small centre of being. Me. My thoughts. My pleasures. My acts. Only me. It is a prison. The world is made up of entirely selfish people. Nothing else matters a damn.' He drank some more. 'I would like to get beyond myself.'

'Shakespeare became other beings,' Ireland said. 'He is the exception. He inhabited their souls. He looked out of their eyes. He spoke from their mouths.'

Charles was now so drunk that he could not follow the conversation. 'Do you believe it to be Shakespeare? It. Mary has shown it to me.'

'*Vortigern?* The play is his. There can be no doubt about it.'

'It cannot be, dear.'

'Why not?' Ireland looked at him defiantly. 'It is his style, is it not? His cadence?'

'I cannot believe –'

'Can you not? Who else might have written it? Name him.' Charles was silent, and drank from his glass with great deliberation. 'No one, you see. You can think of no one.'

'You must be careful with my sister.'

'Careful?'

'Mary is very strange. Very strange. She is attached to you.'

'As I am to her. But there is no – no interest – between us. I have no reason to be careful.'

'So you will give me your word as a gentleman that you have no design upon her.' He stood up, swaying slightly.

'Design upon her? Whatever do you mean by that?'

Charles was not sure what he meant. 'No purpose.'

'What right have you to question me?' Ireland was also very drunk. 'I have no designs or purposes whatsoever.'

'So you give me your word.'

'I will give you nothing of the kind. I resent it. I refute it.' He stood up, to face Charles directly. 'I cannot consider you my friend. I pity your sister. Having such a brother.'

'You pity her, do you? So do I.'

'What do you mean by that?'

'I mean what I choose to mean.' He waved his hand, and accidentally knocked his bottle on to the floor. 'I love my sister, and I pity her.'

'The play *is* Shakespeare's,' de Quincey said.

Chapter Ten

Two days later Richard Brinsley Sheridan entered the book-shop in Holborn Passage.

Samuel Ireland, having been alerted by a scrawled message an hour before, was waiting to greet him. 'My dear sir. An honour.' Sheridan bowed. 'We are all immensely proud.'

'Where is the young man of the hour?' Sheridan was a large figure, and he found it difficult to turn as William descended the staircase. 'Is it you?'

'I am William Ireland, sir.'

'May I shake your hand, sir? You have served a great purpose.' Sheridan announced each word, as if he were addressing others unseen. 'It was Mr Dryden, I believe, who recommended Vortigern as a great subject for a drama.'

'I was not aware of that, sir.'

'Why should you be? His prefaces are not generally known.'

'Alas not.'

'Clearly our bard had anticipated him.' With a flourish Sheridan produced the manuscript from the pocket of his top-coat. 'Your father sent it by hackney last Tuesday. Much obliged.' Sheridan had a keen glance. 'There are bold ideas, sir, even if some are crude and undigested.'

'Sir?' William appeared to be genuinely puzzled.

'Shakespeare must have been a very young man when he wrote this. There is one line –' He put his hand to his fore-head, as if playing Memory. ' *"Under the convex of the wandering heavens, I beg forgiveness of my errant father."* Wandering and errant are too closely laid together. Yet a wandering convex is striking.' William looked at him without saying anything. 'Well I am not a critic, Mr Ireland. I am a man of the theatre. This will fill Drury Lane. A new play by William Shakespeare. Found in the most mysterious circumstances. It will create a sensation.'

'Will you stage it?'

'Drury Lane has read it. Drury Lane esteems it. Drury Lane accepts it.'

'Wonderful news, Father!'

'I see Mr Kemble as Vortigern,' Sheridan continued. 'Such a massive figure on our stage. So imposing. So heavy. And Mrs Siddons as Edmunda? All lightness and grace. What a deli-cious creature she is.'

'May I suggest Mrs Jordan as Suetonia?' William had caught Sheridan's mood. 'I saw her last week in *The Perjured Bride*. She overwhelmed me, Mr Sheridan.'

'You have the soul of an artist, Mr Ireland. You understand us. When I close my eyes, I see Mrs Jordan exactly as Suetonia.' Sheridan did indeed close his eyes. 'And what of Harcourt as Wortimerus? If you had known him in *The Ragged Veil*, he would have frightened you to death. He was tremendous. But do you think –' he hesitated, and looked around at Samuel Ireland – 'do you think we should describe it as "attributed to Shakespeare"? In case of doubt?'

Samuel Ireland took a step backwards, and seemed to stand more upright. 'What possible doubt could there be, Mr Sheridan?'

'A minuscule doubt. A few discrepancies in cadence. A few minor errors in rhyme. A tiny, tiny doubt.'

'There is no doubt at all.'

'If we doubt,' William said, 'then we put out the light.'

'A good image, sir. You have a touch of the bard about you, if I may say so.'

'I have no pretensions as a dramatist, Mr Sheridan.'

'But Shakespeare was probably your age when he wrote this.'

'I cannot say.' William was smiling. 'I do not know.'

'Of course. Nobody knows.' Sheridan turned back to Samuel Ireland. 'My clerk, Mr Dignum, has transcribed the parts. It would be a great honour if you and your son witnessed my *Pizarro* tomorrow night. You must gain some idea of our scale.'

So the Irelands entered Drury Lane the following evening. In the glare of the Argand oil-lamps they mounted the marble steps into the great vestibule with its ceiling covered with the images of Euterpe, the muse of music, Melpomene, the muse of tragedy, and Terpsichore, the muse of dance. Terpsichore herself, painted ten years before by Sir John Hammond, was seen tripping a measure with various cherubs and shepherds.

'Guests of Mr Sheridan!' Samuel Ireland announced his

arrival to the usher, dressed in Drury Lane green, who was not at all inclined to notice him. 'Guests of the manager, Mr Sheridan!'

The usher scratched his wig, silver and powdered, and took the slip of paper. He checked it against a written list pasted upon one of the gilt pillars of the vestibule, and then bowed. ''Amlet Box,' he said. 'Follow me.' He led father and son up the carpet of a staircase resplendent in ebony and gold, and along the first-floor corridor where engravings of Garrick, Betty, Abingdon and others adorned the crimson flock-papered walls.

The Hamlet Box smelled of damp straw and liquorice cordial and cherries. It was the smell of a London theatre. William relished it, just as he relished the odours of perfume and pomade rising in waves from the restless and animated audience. It was the second night of *Pizarro*, a musical drama set in Peru at the time of the Spanish assault against the Incas. When the overture began, its melody bound the audience in the common expectation of enchantment; William felt himself to be dissolved in the haze of light and sound that hung over the auditorium. The drop-curtain was raised to reveal a river, a forest, and a range of mountains topped with snow. The river seemed naturally to flow, and the trees rustled in a breeze that passed over the stage. For William this was more beautiful – more intense, more brightly coloured – than the material world itself. And then the Spanish army marched on stage with pikes and muskets. In his enthusiasm William clapped his hands and leaned over the side of the box to catch a glimpse of Charles Kemble as Pizarro, the Spanish general. The audience was in a state of excitement as the actor walked to the centre of the stage, its cheers and hurrahs heightened by the sudden firing of the muskets by the soldiers.

Kemble gestured with his hands for silence. '*We have come to subjugate a proud and alien race –*'

'This is splendid,' Samuel Ireland whispered to his son. 'Surpasses everything.'

William watched Kemble with fascination. The man had become a Spanish general – not just in appearance and in manner, but in his being. Had he become Pizarro, or had Pizarro become him? The breath of both had become one. William experienced a moment of elation. Here was proof that you might flee the prison of the self. De Quincey had been wrong.

Mrs Siddons now emerged as the Inca princess, Elvira, to prolonged applause. She spoke directly to the audience as if they were her fellow-actors. '*The faith we follow teaches us to live in bonds of charity with all mankind, and die with hope of bliss beyond the grave.*' She recited her lines in a high chant, her hands across her breast in an attitude of spotless rectitude. '*Tell your commanders this and tell them, too, we seek no change. Least of all, such change as you would bring upon us.*'

This was the meaning of the theatre, as William now understood it. It allowed the spectators to rise out of their own selves in an act of communion. Why had he not considered this before? Just as the actors performed this ritual of transformation, becoming more than mere men and women, so the audience attained some higher state of existence and awareness.

An Inca ritual was taking place on stage. Mrs Jordan had emerged, clad in plumes and panther-skins, and was engaged in a dance with Mr Clive Harcourt as Coro. The music of the orchestra came only from the violins; their melody filled Drury Lane with pathos and wonder. William sat back, astonished at the spectacle, and noticed an engraving of Garrick on the side-wall of the box; it was of the actor as Hamlet, contemplating the skull.

Father and son left the theatre elated. They had glimpsed the possibilities for *Vortigern*. 'I see ruins,' Samuel told William. 'I see forests stretching to the horizon.'

'Mr Kemble is very powerful.'

'He has a remarkable voice.'

'Massive feeling. He will make Vortigern great.'

'And a very striking deportment. He quite overwhelmed me.' They were walking north, past Macklin Street and Smart's Gardens. 'You *must* introduce me to your patron, William. I *must* thank her for permitting you – for granting you –'

'The manuscripts were her gift to me. I have told you, Father. She does not wish to be known to the public in any way.'

'But surely to a father –'

'No, sir. Not even to you.'

'I have been considering this very carefully, William. What if some critic – some thankless creature – were to claim that it was not Shakespeare's work?'

'I would deny it.'

'But she would prove your case.'

'Case? There is no case, Father. It will not arise. Anyone who enters Drury Lane, and sees the play, will know it to be Shakespeare's. There will be no doubt about it.'

Samuel Ireland was not entirely convinced. He and Rosa Ponting had often discussed his son's unpredictable behaviour. There were occasions when William would keep to his room for hours at a time without offering any explanation; and, as Rosa discovered, his door was always locked. He would often seem to be awake, and active, all night. She suspected a woman, but could find no evidence of female presence. Since William never permitted either of them to enter his room, it remained a suspicion. When she mentioned it to Samuel, he laughed. 'How could he smuggle her past us, Rosa? Think of it. He cannot be seeing or keeping a woman. Consider the noise. The creaking.' It was true that every sound in William's chamber could be heard in the dining-room below: all they ever heard was the incessant tread of his feet.

'What of Miss Lamb, Sammy? Is that nothing?'

'Miss Lamb is a trusted friend. A customer.'

'Why did he have a fire in the middle of the summer?' They had seen the white smoke coming out of the middle chimney.

Her question did not seem to follow any particular line of thought, and he had no ready answer. 'Really, Rosa, I cannot answer for my son.'

'He is doing something.'

'And what precisely would that be?'

'How am I supposed to know?' She adopted an air of nonchalance. 'It is no concern of mine how your son is occupied.' At that moment William walked upstairs from the bookshop, and their conversation was at an end.

Three days after the performance of *Pizarro*, the Irelands attended a rehearsal of *Vortigern* in the empty auditorium of Drury Lane. They sat upon stools at the side as Charles Kemble and Clive Harcourt paced upon the stage. Harcourt, slim and delicate of feature, had been cast as Wortimerus.

> *'In deep betrayal steeped I come before you,*
> *Father, seeking the mercy of your blessed hand.'*

The actor had seemed so slight, so unworthy of attention, that William was amazed how suddenly he came to life; it was as if he had been visited by some unseen power. He actually seemed to grow taller. Kemble, thick-set and orotund, had become Vortigern.

> *'Time was, alas, I needed not this plea*
> *But here's a secret and a stinging thorn*
> *That wounds my troubled nerves – O son, O son,*
> *By boldly thrusting on thee dire ambition*
> *If there is aught of malice in the plot*
> *'Twas I who led you to deep-dyed betrayal.'*

He stopped, dissatisfied with his rendering. 'Should I not suggest, Sheridan, that the son carries more blame than the father?' His voice was still that of Vortigern. 'The son murdered his uncle to please his father. That is so. But should the father then blame himself?' He looked towards William, for some assistance in the matter.

'The father urged him on,' William said. 'He would not have conceived the plot without his father's presence.'

'His presence? That is very interesting.' He walked to the front of the stage, and looked out over the darkened auditorium. A few shafts of light came from the lantern of the dome, winking and glimmering with particles of dust. 'I must convey my presence, even when I am off the stage?' He turned back to Sheridan. 'Is it possible?'

'Anything, for you, is possible.'

'I could be heard laughing. Or singing perhaps. My voice would carry from the wings.'

'Vortigern does not sing, sir.' William ventured his opinion very quietly.

'Surely you could write a song, Mr Ireland? Some old English ballad will suit.'

'I am not a writer, Mr Kemble.'

'Oh no? I have seen you in *Westminster Words*.'

William seemed flattered that his essays had been noticed by so great a personage. 'I could perhaps invent a verse, if you so –'

'Make it Shakespearian. Stirring. Something to do with the clash of arms and the flight of ravens. You know the sort of thing.'

Mrs Siddons, taking the role of Edmunda, was growing impatient. 'If Mr Kemble is prepared, we might try a little more of the original.' She was of relatively short stature but, when she spoke, she seemed to William to be a large woman; her voice preceded her, as it were, and warned people that she was coming. 'I always think it a mistake to depart from the actual words. Don't you?'

It was not clear whom she was addressing, but Kemble came up to her. 'We are ready for you, Sarah.'

She took up her part, and began to read.

> *Enough. You both are judged aright*
> *Of fouling name, and fame, and your dear country.*
> *The sentence will be swift and sudden*
> *Upon so bold and dark a plot.*
> *Never was maze more tortuous.'*

'Sarah, dear. You have something in your hair.'

She put her hands up to her head, and a moth fluttered away. Harcourt burst into laughter, went down on one knee, and then rolled upon the stage.

She looked at him with distaste. 'For a small man,' she said, 'you make a deal of noise.'

The rehearsals continued until late in the afternoon, when Mrs Siddons declared that she would 'drop' without camomile tea. William was still in high spirits, however. The words he had previously seen only in manuscript had taken on the dimensions of the human world. They had become feelings, enlarged or tentative as the actors had judged them.

He left the theatre that evening with his father; they were both walking quickly, as if to keep pace with their own thoughts, when William almost collided with a tall young man about to cross Catherine Street. He recognised him at once. He had met him in the Salutation and Cat, on the night when he and Charles had argued. 'Good Lord, I know you,' he said. 'Charles has introduced us.'

'Drinkwater, sir. Siegfried Drinkwater.'

Ireland introduced him to his father, who bowed to the young man and professed himself honoured and gratified by his acquaintance.

'And how is Pyramus and Thisbe?'

'Have you not heard? It is cancelled.'

'Why?'

'Miss Lamb is very unwell. She cannot leave her room.'

'What?' William had heard nothing from the Lambs. He regretted his quarrel with Charles; he could not remember how it began, but he recalled the intensity of his drunken passion. 'What is the matter with her?'

'It is some kind of fever. Charles is not sure.'

'I know the cause. She never recovered from her fall.' He was addressing his father. 'By accident she slipped into the Thames. I told you.'

'Well,' Siegfried said. 'It is farewell to Snout and to Flute.'

The next morning William walked into Laystall Street, at a time when he knew Charles would be at business.

The door was opened by Tizzy who, on seeing him, gave a peculiar titter. 'Oh is it you, Mr Ireland? You have been a stranger.'

'I had no notion that Miss Lamb was ill. I came as soon as –'

'She is poorly still. But she is sitting up. Please to wait downstairs.'

When he walked into the drawing-room he saw Mr Lamb sitting cross-legged on the Turkey rug. 'Beware the watchman,' the old man told him. 'The watchman comes when no one knows.'

'I beg your pardon, sir?'

'It arrives in the night. It is the work of ages.' He lapsed into silence.

A few moments later Tizzy appeared. 'She will be down directly, Mr Ireland.'

'Please not for my sake. If she is still unwell –'

'She needs the change.'

When Mary entered the room, William realised that there had been an alteration in her. She seemed much calmer, as if she were intent upon some inner purpose. She greeted William with a light kiss upon his cheek, a gesture that astonished him. Tizzy had already turned away, and had not seen it. Mr Lamb folded his arms, rocking backwards and forwards on the rug.

'It has been a long time, William, since you visited.'

'I had no notion that you were indisposed.'

'Indisposed? Nothing of the kind. I have been resting.'

'Of course.'

'But it is good of you to call. Father and I often talk of you. Don't we, Pa?' Mr Lamb looked at his daughter fearfully, and said nothing. 'You must have some tea. Tizzy!' The maid stopped, turned, and came back into the room. 'Tea for our guest, please.' Her voice was stern, implacable. 'Do sit down, William. Talk to me about something.'

He was unnerved and embarrassed by her. 'The play is in rehearsal at Drury Lane. Kemble plays Vortigern.'

'Oh yes? Charles will be pleased to hear of it.' She seemed distracted, scarcely listening to what he was saying. 'Where is that tea, I wonder? It is so like Tizzy. She is always in a muddle. I wonder that you put up with her, Pa.' Mr Lamb continued rocking backward and forward. 'You have heard that Charles has prevented us from playing Pyramus and Thisbe? It is too bad of him.'

'I met Mr Drinkwater in the street.'

'You met Flute, did you? Poor Flute. He has no music.'

William did not know how to reply. 'I will be sending your family tickets.'

'Tickets?'

'For *Vortigern*, Miss Lamb.'

'Oh why do you not call me Mary?'

She burst into tears.

William looked on, horrified, as Tizzy hurried back into the room. 'Well, Miss, it was not good to leave your bed was it? You have caught a chill, and now you are paying for it.' She gestured to William that he should leave and, with a helpless glance at Mr Lamb sitting on the rug, he went out of the door.

Chapter Eleven

It was the first night of *Vortigern*. Drury Lane was filled to its capacity, from box to pit. From a gap between the wing and the drop-curtain William could pick out the faces of those he knew. Close to the stage were Charles and Mary Lamb, together with their father. In the Hamlet Box were Samuel Ireland, Rosa Ponting and Edmond Malone. Tom Coates and Benjamin Milton were standing together in the pit, but William could see Selwyn Onions and Siegfried Drinkwater behind them. Thomas de Quincey had just come through a side-entrance, and was looking for a place. The Macbeth Box was occupied by two Members of Parliament, with their wives, while the Othello Box had been given to Kemble's large family. In the Lear Box was the Earl of Kilmartin with his mistress. The whole of London seemed to have arrived. William could not bear to join them; he had decided to remain back-stage out of sheer fright. He could no more have seen the play as part of the audience than he could have performed in it himself. It was too close to him.

The area behind the drop-curtain was filled with activity. The master of the stage was moving a large boulder into a more central position, while the senior property man was adjusting the branches of an artificial tree. The scene represented a woodland glade in an ancient British forest, and a number of stage-workers were busily placing bushes and moss-covered rocks over the wooden boards. A moon was being hauled into position by means of a rope and pulley, prompting the master of the stage to sing out the old favourite of the song-and-supper rooms, 'Why Are There No Monkeys on the Moon?' In a gush of recollection William remembered his father singing it, in a rowing-boat near Hammersmith; it was a hot afternoon, and he could smell his father's sweat as he laboured at the oars.

'It will be a grand night, Mr Ireland.' Sheridan was standing just behind him, in the shade of a gnarled oak-tree. 'I have high hopes.'

'Will the audience be with us, do you think?'

'Of course. What Englishman could fail to rise to a new Shakespearian play? They will cheer, Mr Ireland. They will hurrah. They may even call for the author.'

'But the author will not be forthcoming.'

'A jest, sir. But you may take a bow as first finder.'

'Oh no. Unthinkable.'

'Not even to explain the circumstances of your discovery?'

'I could not, Mr Sheridan. I cannot.' Ireland seemed to be genuinely frightened by Sheridan's suggestion. 'I have no words for such an audience. It is too – too imposing.'

'Very well, Mr Ireland. You may keep to the dressing-area, if you wish. It will fall to me to speak on your behalf. A young man who by great good fortune has come upon an assemblage of Shakespeare's hitherto unknown and unseen papers, et cetera. Wonderful stuff. I might turn it into an epilogue for a later performance. Will this do?' He struck an attitude.

> ' "Words, once my stock, are wanting to commend
> Our greatest poet, and his bold young friend.
> Shakespeare and Ireland now together stand
> And earn the plaudits of a grateful land."

'Do you think it fit?'
  'And then, sir, you might add –

> "Now where are the successors to his name?
> What bring they to fill out a poet's fame?
> Weak, short-lived issues of a feeble age
> Scarce living to be christened on the stage."'

'You have a gift, Mr Ireland. But we must not complain about the feeble age. It will not be good for business. We may condemn the critics instead. How is this?

> "And malice in all critics reigns so high
> That for small errors they whole plays decry."'

William continued his verse for him.

> ' "You equal judges of the whole will be,
> They judge but half who only faults will see."'

'Congratulations, Mr Ireland. You are a poet.'

'I have no such ambitions, sir.'

'Nonsense. One day you will write a play. I know it.'

The master of the stage came up to Sheridan, and described the properties as 'captivating' and 'astonishing'. 'This will melt them, Mr Sheridan. This is sylvan. This is yesteryear.'

'Have you left room for Kemble to flourish?'

'He has a plateau of rock.'

'And Mrs Siddons? I worry about her wig against these branches. You recall the disaster in *The Twins of Tottenham*?'

'She will not be snagged. I have arranged them high.'

'And there is still stage enough for the warriors? With their spears and shields?'

'They will be terrifying, sir. They have been painted with woad. One of the water-colourists has done them.'

It was time now for the stage to be cleared of all its workers, its wardrobe-keepers and stage-hands, its dressers and scene-painters. William walked behind the scenes to the back-stage area where the warriors were already assembled; they were known in the theatre as 'the walking gentlemen' with no lines of their own. There was much subdued whispering and chattering, hushed by strains of music as the orchestra commenced the overture especially written by the conductor, Crispin Bank. It was entitled 'Vortigern's Dream'. Charles Kemble approached the darkened wings in his costume. He was wearing a tartan kilt together with a bronze breast-plate and a silver helmet surmounted by pink and blue plumes. He glanced at William but did not seem to see him; he was fixed in the role of Vortigern. He cleared his throat and looked up at all the stage machinery. At the other side of the stage Mrs Siddons was being larded with grease and powder. The overture was complete. The audience became quiet. William retreated further back, among discarded stools and properties. He could not endure this silence.

The drop-curtain rose, creaking, to a chorus of cheers and hurrahs that took William by surprise. The audience was cheering the scenery. After a few moments he could hear Vortigern's voice distinctly, as he berated his daughter for becoming secretly betrothed to the Roman general Constantius. Mrs Siddons, swathed in draperies dating from no particular period, took up her position centre-stage. With arms outstretched, just blocking Kemble from the general view of the audience, she recited the virtues of her lover.

> 'No brow so rough but sure will smooth at his,
> No frown so black but will to sweetness turn
> And, bright as sun when bursting from the east,
> Drives night away. Yet why entreat I thus?'

William could detect approval from the audience; there was a palpable sense of content, even of surprise, at the quality of the verse. Towards the end of the first act, Mrs Siddons burst into song.

> 'Last Whitsuntide they brought me
> Roses and lilies fair;
> Violets too they gave me,
> To bind my golden hair.'

There was laughter from the pit, at the mention of her hair colour, but she continued in a clear unfaltering voice. When she came off at the end of the act, however, William saw that she was in tears; she ran into the arms of her dresser, an elderly woman known only as 'Crump', and was led back into the green-room.

The mood of the audience had changed by the opening of the second act. Vortigern was upon the stage eager to rally his troops before their battle against the Romans. It was a long speech that at its end included a stern apostrophe to Death as a way of stirring the assembled soldiers:

> *'O then thou dost ope wide thy hideous jaws*
> *And with rude laughter and fantastic tricks*
> *Thou clasps thy rattling fingers to their side*
> *And when this solemn mockery is over —'*

After this line had been delivered, William heard a single howl of derision rising from the pit. Once it had been expressed, it became infectious. Kemble tried the line again. Now, the whole audience was overcome with laughter. After two or three minutes Kemble resumed his speech.

> *And when this solemn mockery is over,*
> *We will —'*

The audience could not be controlled. To William's amazement there was a general and prolonged hysteria that lasted for several minutes. He could hear a thudding sound that he interpreted, correctly, as the noise of fruit being thrown upon the stage.

William became very calm, almost indifferent. He studied the palm of his hand with intense concentration, wondering if there was some slight break or diversion in his line of life.

The actors struggled through the rest of the second act, interrupted by occasional laughter and hoots of derision. Mrs Jordan stalked upon the stage in her best classical manner, with one stride followed by a short step. She waved her hands mysteriously before her face, as if she were peering through a veil at some object far off – prompting a call from one member of the audience that 'He's over here!' She had insisted on wearing white muslin, as became a Roman matron, but half-way across the stage one corner of it became entangled with a bush. Mr Harcourt knelt down, in the pretence of picking some of its leaves, in order to release her costume. Harcourt was well known also as a comic actor, and could not resist pulling some of his most famous 'comical faces'. For this production he gave what he called his 'Roman orgy face', a mixture of lust and cynicism and weariness that he managed with his mouth turned down and his eyebrows turned up. It was much appreciated by the audience, on the many occasions he repeated it.

The battle between the Romans and the Britons, in the third act, was not altogether a success. The woad had begun to run on the skins of the ancient Britons, and in the desperate hand-to-hand combat it was liberally smeared over the faces and wooden armour of the Roman infantry. As one of the walking gentlemen said later, 'We looked like parrots.' In that battle Mr Harcourt fell mortally wounded just as the drop-curtain was about to be lowered; unfortunately he had so placed himself on stage that the curtain literally divided his body. His head and shoulders faced the actors on stage, while his lower half was visible to the audience. He struggled to free himself since, as he said to Mrs Siddons later, 'I could not lie there dying all evening.' But the uproar of laughter could be heard as far as Bow Street and Covent Garden.

William remained impassive even when Sheridan approached him. 'I thought Shakespeare had written a tragedy. He seems to have written a comedy.'

'I am at a loss for words, sir.'

'*You*? Oh surely not?'

'I really do not know what to say.'

'Nothing. Nothing in the world, Mr Ireland. It is not the most subtle humour. But it has had the desired effect. I congratulate you.'

'There is no reason whatever to praise me, Mr Sheridan.'

'Every reason. You have given us – how shall I put it – a novelty!'

'It was not of my devising. Shakespeare –'

'Is a very good name on the play-bill. We will keep it.'

'We will have a run?'

'As long as the English public retains its humour.'

The last two acts proceeded more quietly; there was occasional laughter but there was also applause after some of the soliloquies. In the final scene Vortigern and Edmunda are reunited among the slain of both sides. Kemble and Mrs Siddons stood beside each other, clearly exhausted by the events of the evening, and clasped hands in a gesture of mutual forgiveness before they sank upon the stage and expired. Mrs Siddons began:

> *As I kiss thee, methinks sweet love himself*
> *Sits on thy front and waves thy silvery hair.'*

To which Kemble replied:

> *'You smile as if an angel kissed your lips,*
> *And whispered you of joys that are to come.'*

When the drop-curtain finally came down there was applause and cheering mingled with a few boos and cat-calls. The cast assembled on the stage as the curtain rose again, and took a general bow. As a large bouquet of lilies was presented to Mrs Siddons, there were cries of 'Author! Author!' which caused much laughter in the pit. When the curtain came down again, after a stirring performance of the national anthem from actors and audience, Mrs Siddons hurried off to the green-room without glancing at William Ireland. Kemble came up to him, however, and put his arm round him. 'We survived, sir. We hit choppy waters, and we were holed beneath the deck, but we sailed on guns blazing! God bless the London stage!'

William still felt strangely indifferent to the night's proceedings. The fear and the shock, upon hearing the first notes of ridicule, had left him. He was very tired.

Samuel Ireland and Rosa Ponting were waiting for him in the corridor that led from the back of the stage to the green-room. 'I know what it is to be proud,' his father said. 'You have exceeded all expectation.'

'Quite a treat.' Rosa Ponting was looking at him with an expression of curiosity and sympathy. 'Don't pay attention to them that laughed.'

'Nothing,' Samuel Ireland said. 'A trifle. A deliberate claque.'

'The Lambs came up to your father and congratulated him.'

'The Lambs?' William had already forgotten that he had seen them in the auditorium; it seemed a long age ago.

'Charles and Mary were standing by the orchestra. With a funny old gentleman. They looked up and saw us. We had such a nice box to ourselves. Everyone was watching your father.'

'Where is Sheridan?' his father was asking. 'I must shake his hand. He is the great begetter. There must be a celebration. Some toasts.'

'Forgive me, Father. Do stay and greet Mr Sheridan. I will walk back.'

Samuel Ireland needed no prompting to linger in the passages of the theatre; Rosa, dressed in a satin and lace gown lovingly prepared by her dress-maker and confidante in Harley Street, was eager to meet Mrs Siddons and Mrs Jordan. So William left Drury Lane alone. As he passed the corner of Catherine Street and Tavistock Street he noticed a man in a shabby hat and frock-coat giving out handbills to those who were coming from the theatre; he was restless and eager, darting between the small pockets of people and thrusting the paper into their hands. He approached William who, taking the bill, saw the black type of 'RANK FORGERY' at its head.

William stopped and addressed him. 'Who are you, sir?'

'A lover of Shakespeare, sir.'

'And you do not love this play?'

'Oh no. Fraudulent, sir. A fakery.'

'How do you know that?'

'I have a friend in the theatre who showed it to me.' William suspected that the man himself was an out-of-work actor. 'It never has the genuine note.'

'I disagree with you. I have just seen it. I assure you it is real.'

'Ah, sir, it may be real and yet unreal. Do you understand me?'

He rushed upon another group before William could ask

him what he meant. So William walked towards Covent Garden, clutching the handbill, until he caught a glimpse of the Lambs a few yards in front of him. Mary Lamb was walking arm in arm with her father, talking intently to him. William did not wish to be noticed, so he held back until they had entered the cobbled space of the market itself. Then he saw Mary walking quickly away, towards that part of the arcade where the potters kept their stalls, with Charles following her. Had there been some disagreement between them?

He turned away and walked back towards Holborn. That night, he slept profoundly and awoke the next morning much later than his usual hour.

Chapter Twelve

Thomas de Quincey also possessed a copy of the handbill that had been distributed outside the Drury Lane Theatre. He had been given it, as a memento of that night, by Charles Lamb. De Quincey and Lamb were now very friendly; they had become drinking companions, and Charles had assisted him in finding a junior clerk's post at South Sea House in Threadneedle Street. De Quincey had a good hand, having attended the grammar school in Manchester, and was surprisingly numerate. They met on many evenings, after work, in the Billiter Inn. It was here that Charles showed him the handbill, five nights after the first performance of *Vortigern*.

'Our friend is accused of "rank forgery",' he said with a certain relish.

'Is he so?'

'But Ireland could not have written so much. He could not

have written so fluently. It was excellent poetry in parts. You were there.' He touched de Quincey's arm. 'I have a theory. I believe this play to have been written by some contemporary of Shakespeare's. Some minor poet, perhaps. Ireland is so seduced by the name of Shakespeare that he attaches it to every item he has found.'

'I think more highly of him than you do.'

'It is the work of Shakespeare?'

'On the contrary. It is the work of Ireland.'

'That cannot be. How could he fool the world?'

'London, at least. He is far more clever than you imagine, Charles. When I hear him talk I am always aware of his incisive nature. He is very sharp.'

'But to write a sixteenth-century play – and poetry. Surely not?'

'Chatterton accomplished as much. And he was even younger. It is not impossible.'

'Improbable. Highly improbable.'

'He can write. You have seen his essays. Mr Ireland may be deeper than you suppose.'

'I must tell Mary your theory.'

'Oh no.' De Quincey was very emphatic. 'On no account tell Mary.'

'I know what you are about to say.'

'Listen to me all the same. She is too – too fragile at the moment.' De Quincey sought the right phrase. 'It might break her.'

'Break her heart, do you mean? Nonsense.'

'Really, Charles, sometimes you do not see what is under your nose.'

'I cannot see what is not there.'

'Mary is there. Can you not see that she is pining for him? Her illness? Her nervousness? William Ireland has deeply unsettled her. And he has no intention of doing anything about it.'

If Charles was surprised by de Quincey's description, he did not show it. Mary's fits of temper, and her evident unease, had become more pronounced in recent weeks. But Charles had explained this to himself as the strain of their father's advancing senility. He knew that she was protective of Ireland – and even regarded him with affection – but secretly to love him? 'So she is Ophelia,' he said. 'Wasting.'

'Why must you see everything as drama, Charles? Mary is not a character in a play. She is suffering.' He was silent for a moment. 'Ireland forges his feelings as he forges words.'

'And that is why I cannot explain your theory to her.'

'Better if you did not.'

De Quincey walked back from the Billiter Inn to his lodging in Berners Street. He had taken a room close to the abandoned house where he had first lived, because he had not lost hope of finding Anne in the crowded streets of that neighbourhood. Once he thought he saw her, sitting by the corner of Newman Street, but when he hurried to that spot there was no one there. He imagined her consumed in sorrow and in loneliness; he imagined her walking into the Thames; he imagined her abused and beaten. Oh for a muse of fire – to cast a light into London's darkness! These were the words that came to him when, suddenly, he glimpsed William Ireland entering the stationer's shop at the bottom of Berners Street. The hour was late but Ireland had opened the door without knocking;

de Quincey passed the shop-front very quickly and stole a glance through the bay window on the ground floor. The elderly man behind the counter was handing Ireland a parcel. That was all he had time to witness.

He walked on, and entered the house where he lodged. Despite his warnings to Charles, de Quincey remained on friendly terms with Ireland. In certain respects he even admired him. He considered him to be a fine actor, whose stage was the world, but he was the first to admit that he did not properly understand him.

He was about to enter his room when there was a knock on the front door. Ireland was on the doorstep, clutching the parcel wrapped in rough brown paper. 'I saw you passing,' he said. 'You did not notice me.'

'Where were you?'

'In Askew's. He gives me the Zurich catalogue. Charming old fellow.'

'Come in, sir playwright. I have a bottle that desires your company.' De Quincey's room was on the ground floor, looking on to Berners Street itself.

'I am not the playwright, Tom. I am the medium.'

'I know it. You are what mathematicians call the middle term, without which there can be no lower or upper.'

'And the play is the upper term?'

'So long as Shakespeare is not the lower. Mind the rent in the carpet.'

De Quincey's room was bare of ornament; there was a bed, and many books piled on the carpet, but very little else. The traffic of London passed by the window, and the continuous low sound of the city could clearly be heard.

'I have often wondered where you lodged,' Ireland said.

'I like it here.' De Quincey was very jaunty. 'I feel myself to be a Londoner. Let me open that bottle.'

'I have lived in the city all my life. There are some spots that I love. But I have no real passion for it.'

'Why ever not? It has made you.'

'And may yet break me.' William went over to the window, and looked out at the crossing-sweeper who worked the entire street. 'The play closes tonight.'

'*Vortigern?*'

'Six nights. I thought it would go on –'

'Surely not?'

Ireland turned round. 'What do you mean?'

De Quincey was momentarily at a loss. 'Shakespeare is an acquired taste. He is not for a modern audience.'

'Yet we have had our defenders. I cut this from the *Evening Gazette.*' He took a paper out of his pocket, and read from it aloud.

> 'From deep oblivion snatched, this play appears.
> It claims respect, since Shakespeare's name it bears.
> That name, the source of wonder and delight,
> To a fair hearing has at least a right.'

De Quincey laughed. 'A very lamentable set of verses.'

'I agree. I could have written better myself.' Ireland looked carefully at him. 'But the sentiment is just.'

'Of course.'

Ireland seemed reassured. 'I will tell you something, Tom, that few others know. I can trust your silence.' De Quincey gave the briefest nod. 'Among the vast stock of papers, given to me by my patron, I have found another Henry.'

'I beg your pardon?'

'*Henry II.* Is that not extraordinary?'

De Quincey went over to a walnut box beside his bed, and took out a bottle of Maconochie port. There was a pitcher and wash-stand on the other side of his bed; he crossed over and took out two glasses from the cabinet at its base. He noticed for the first time that the enamel on the side of the basin had chipped and darkened. 'Have you shown it to anyone?'

'My father has seen it. He has passed the sheets to Mr Malone, who has already identified it as the work of the bard.'

'Has anyone else read the manuscript?'

'No one else. Not yet. We are waiting for the propitious time. When the true worth of *Vortigern* is realised. Shall we have a toast?'

De Quincey poured out the port, and they raised their glasses.

'To Henry,' Ireland said.

'To Henry. May the best man win.'

'What is that?'

'A phrase. Nothing.'

'My father wished to see it published. But I have counselled him to wait. Coming so soon after *Vortigern* –'

'It would seem too fortuitous?'

'Precisely. There is a line in *Pericles* about a great sea of joys rushing upon him.'

'*O'erbear the shores of my mortality.* Is that right? *And drown me with their sweetness.*'

'You know it. But there are some who say that *Pericles* is not by Shakespeare.'

'Some will say anything.'

'That is my dilemma.' Ireland finished his port quickly. 'May I?' He sat down upon the edge of the bed. 'The press of visitors has become so great,' he said after de Quincey had filled his glass, 'that my father has printed cards of admission. Our little museum has become a shrine, as he predicted. Did I tell you? The Prince of Wales appeared one morning.'

'No!'

'All dressed up in powder-blue silk. Old Corruption himself. Some addle-headed courtier rushed in, telling us to prepare ourselves. What were we supposed to do? Put on court costume? Then his fat Highness waddled in. My father bowed so low that you could see up his –' Ireland broke into laughter. 'I will not say.'

'But what did the prince do?'

'He called for the papers, sat himself down on a chair that the courtier found for him, and then – in his word – "perused" them for a minute or two. The shop was filled with the stink of his cologne-water.'

'And what did he say of them?'

'I will give you his precise words.' Although de Quincey did not know it, Ireland imitated the voice and the manner of the Prince of Wales exactly. '"These documents bear a strong semblance of age. But to decide peremptorily, from this cursory inspection, would be unjustifiable." And then my father replies thus. "Of course it would. Unthinkable, gracious sir."'

'And then?'

'"I trust," his Fatness says, "I trust the English nation will experience that gratification which is expected to be derived from them."'

'What did that mean?'

'God knows. My father told me later that royalty can venture no opinion. I begged to differ, citing the American wars.'

'Did he stay long?'

'Not at all. He got up to leave and my father fluttered around him. Gracious sir. Privilege not dreamed of. Ardent zeal. And so forth. As soon as he had left, my father kissed the chair, and vowed that no one would ever sit in it again.'

'But you were not so impressed.'

'Impressed? With that charlatan? I would prefer to bow to this crossing-sweep. He has more natural dignity.'

'And he has employment.'

'Precisely.' William put down his glass, and picked up the parcel he had brought with him from Askew's. 'I must get back. I do not trust the streets between here and Holborn.'

His father was waiting for his return. He was standing behind the counter, and William knew at once that he was ill at ease.

'They have established a committee of inquiry,' Samuel said.

'I beg your pardon, Father?'

'A committee of inquiry. Into your papers.'

'I had thought that they were ours. What committee?'

'Mr Stevens and Mr Ritson, both enemies of Mr Malone, have persuaded others to join them in an investigation of all the material you have found. I have been sent a letter by Mr Malone, outlining their malice and their desire to ruin his reputation.'

'His reputation? What about mine? And yours?' Samuel Ireland flinched. 'This is outrageous. Appalling. They are practically telling the world that they suspect us of false dealing.' William burst out laughing. 'As if that were possible.'

'There is no reason for laughter.'

'But there is *need*, Father. How else am I to respond?'

'Surely you see it? You must produce your patron.'

'Why should I entertain the least regard for these gentlemen? They are nothing to me.'

'They are everything. They will be your judge and your jury. You must take them to the source of these papers.'

'It cannot be done.'

'I am sorry to press you, William, but the greater world must be considered. You owe it to the English public. These papers are their birthright.'

'I have told you. My patron will not be named or known. She has given me these papers under the strictest injunctions of secrecy. How do I know that, in the presence of these gentlemen, she might deny all knowledge of me and my proceedings? Think of that, Father.'

'You must persuade —'

'She is not open to persuasion.'

'Consider the consequences to me, William.'

'You knew, Father, on what terms I gave you the documents.'

'You are very cruel to a parent.'

'No. Very honest.' William climbed the stairs and retired to bed.

On the following morning a letter was delivered to W. H. Ireland Esquire. It came from Mr Ritson and politely enquired if Mr Ireland would be willing to answer questions that had occurred to certain learned gentlemen on their examination of the recent papers attributed to Mr William Shakespeare? They also hoped to question Mr Edmond Malone and Mr Samuel Ireland —

'It is abominable to insert my name in this,' Samuel Ireland interjected.

– in the course of their inquiries, which were to be conducted without the slightest suspicion of censoriousness or blame. They hoped that Mr William Ireland would accept the invitation in the spirit with which it was intended, viz., that of open and unrestricted debate.

'I think nothing of their syntax,' William said after he had finished reading the letter aloud to his father. 'They are strangling their own words.'

'Guilty consciences generally give that impression. Lady Macbeth.'

'She sinned out of ambition, not jealousy. What fools these people are. They are not interested in proving or disproving anything. They want to destroy.'

'What will you write in reply?'

'What do you suggest, Father?'

'Suggest? I have nothing to suggest. I gave you my advice last night. I have nothing more to say.'

'Then I will ignore them. I will rise above them.'

This resolution was tested on the following day when the *Pall Mall Review* carried a paragraph, with the heading 'SHAKESPEARE AND IRELAND'; it adverted to 'the sins of the father' being carried by 'the unfortunate son' and adduced the parable of Abraham and Isaac. The item concluded, 'Will this committee be served up the sacrifice of young Ireland on the altar of his father's ambitions?'

'This is intolerable!' Samuel Ireland threw down the journal. 'Why is the odium being heaped upon *my* head?'

'I cannot imagine, Father.'

'This is not fair. Not just. I have never met your patron. I have never seen the house in which the papers are kept.'

Rosa Ponting had come down the staircase, and was quietly listening. 'What are they accusing you of, Sammy?'

'They are accusing me, Rosa, of fabricating the Shakespearian papers.'

'Oh surely not, Father. They merely suspect you of using them —'

'I do not think so, William. There is a clear suggestion that I am a forger and a felon.'

'Heaven forbid!' Rosa already had visions of the jail and the gallows. 'Sammy a criminal person!'

'It will not come to that, Rosa.' William seemed determined to remain calm.

'Not if you do your bounden duty, William Ireland. You must tell them everything.'

'Why must I be put in the dock?' He turned to his father. 'I did not ask you to show the papers to Mr Malone. Or to Mr Sheridan. I was content for them gradually to be sent into the world. You were the one who brought down the whirlwind of public knowledge.'

'You cannot talk to your father in this way.' Rosa was very stern. 'He is already bowed down.'

'I am only speaking the truth. Let me ask you this, Father, out of curiosity. Suppose, sir, they should not be the real manuscripts of William Shakespeare?'

'Impossible.' Samuel Ireland shook his head. 'If the supposed forger stood before me now and confessed, I would not believe him.'

'Is that your solemn opinion and judgement?'

'The documents are too voluminous. They bear all the impressions of their time.'

'Well. I was merely putting the case. And it is decided. Knowing our innocence, I shall write to Mr Ritson expressing my pleasure in acceding to his request.'

'And what of your poor father?' Rosa asked him. 'He deserves consideration, does he not?'

'When I present myself before these gentlemen, I will exonerate him of all blame.'

'Blame?'

'Responsibility.'

'See this, Mary.' Charles Lamb folded the newspaper and, across the breakfast table, passed his sister a paragraph of news concerning William Ireland's forthcoming appearance before the committee.

She read it quickly. 'This is persecution.' She dropped her cup into its saucer, startling her father. 'Is William to be questioned and traduced by anyone who proclaims himself an authority?' Charles was surprised by her vehemence. In recent weeks she seemed to have lost all interest in William Ireland. She had become very calm and quiet. 'Who can possibly doubt that they are genuine works? Will you write to him, Charles, expressing our support?'

'I am not sure that he needs –'

'Very well. I will do it. If you have not the decency to demonstrate loyalty to a friend, I will take your place.' She rose from the table. 'I will write to him now. This instant.'

Mr Lamb looked across at her. 'No jam today. Jam tomorrow.'

'Do not excite yourself, Mr Lamb.' Mrs Lamb looked at her daughter with something like distaste. 'Do sit down, Mary. Charles will be happy to write to Mr Ireland, I am sure.'

'You cannot speak for Charles.'

'Tizzy! More hot water.'

'Did you hear me, Ma?'

'I always hear you, Mary. Sometimes I wish I did not.'

'Of course I will write to him.' Charles was alarmed by his sister's stridency. 'I will tell him that we are concerned.'

Mary sat down as Tizzy brought in the pot. 'And you must tell him that we believe wholly in the authenticity of the papers.'

'Must I?'

'It is of the utmost importance.'

Mrs Lamb looked quickly at her son. 'It can do no harm, Charles. And it will please your sister.' Mary began polishing the butter knife with her shawl. 'Are you sure, Mary, that is polite?'

'I have been reading Boethius, Ma. *The Consolation of Philosophy.*'

'Whatever has that to do with it?'

'Politeness is a mere game. We must live in the eternal world.'

'God willing, we will do. But we do not dwell there as yet.'

Charles, believing that the storm had subsided, took up the newspaper and came upon an account of a recent murder in the White Hart Inn. The victim had been an elderly laundress, whose body was found upturned in a beer barrel; the killer had not been caught. He began reading this narrative aloud, but Mary stopped him.

'I cannot bear this violence,' she said. 'Wherever I go in London, I see barbarism and cruelty.'

'Cities are places of death, Mary.' He harboured some imp of the perverse, with which he still liked to tease his sister. 'I read recently that the first cities were built upon graveyards.'

'So we are the walking dead. Did you hear that, Pa?'

Mr Lamb imitated the sound of a trumpet, and laughed.

Chapter Thirteen

William Ireland was summoned before the Shakespeare Committee a week after he had sent his acceptance of its invitation. It was convened on Sunday morning in the room above a coffee-house in Warwick Lane; it was the office of the Caledonian Society, and various engravings of the Highland regiments adorned the walls. He had arrived with his father, who waited for him on the landing outside the door. Samuel Ireland had immediately called for coffee, toast and brandy wine from the establishment below and, just as William was about to give his testimony, he opened the door a fraction so that he might hear the proceedings.

Mr Ritson and Mr Stevens sat side by side behind a narrow table of oak. Mr Ritson was an eager and animated man, much given to pulling facial expressions of astonishment or disbelief; he was no more than thirty-five, at William's guess, and wore his cravat fashionably knotted. Mr Stevens was older and of a more severe appearance; he looked, William said later, as if he were about to drown several puppies. Two other men were sitting beside them, one of whom began scribbling notes as soon as William entered the room. The room itself smelt of ink and dust, with the faintest savour of pears.

'I would like to make an exact and correct statement before we begin.' William stood in front of them, having refused the offer of a chair, and looked out of a small mullioned window at the dome of St Paul's.

'We are not a court of law, Mr Ireland.' Ritson spread out his hands, as if he were pleading with him. 'We are simply conducting an inquiry. There are no rewards and no punishments.'

'I am glad to hear it. But my father believes that he is being punished.'

'Wherefore?'

'He is suspected of basely forging these documents. Is that not so?'

'He has been accused of nothing.'

'That is not what I said. Suspected, not accused.'

'The world is filled with suspicions.' Stevens had been looking at William very carefully, but now broke his silence. 'We are not perfect, Mr Ireland. We are frail. We have not even concluded that the papers are fabrications. We do not know.'

'You have the opportunity,' Ritson added, 'to dispel any slight cloud.'

'Then I must make my statement.'

'Before you do so, Mr Ireland, will you answer a question? It is very brief.'

'Certainly.'

Ritson laid his hands on the table in front of him. 'William Henry Ireland, will you make oath that to the best of your knowledge and belief, from every circumstance that you know respecting the discovery of these papers, that they are genuine effusions from the pen of William Shakespeare?'

'Forgive me. Do I have leave to read my statement?'

'Of course.'

William took a step backwards, and produced a paper from the inside pocket of his jacket. 'It has been stated in the public prints that the present committee has been appointed to investigate my father's concern in the discovery and presentation of the Shakespearian documents. In order to ease him from the lies surrounding him, I therefore will make oath that he received the papers from me as Shakespeare's own and knows nothing of the origin and source from whence they come.' He returned the paper to his pocket. 'Is that sufficient?'

'Sufficient for your father,' Stevens replied. 'But you have not answered our original question. May we ask about your own part in this?'

'Certainly.'

'Can you enlighten us, then, on the nature of this origin or source?'

'Could you be more precise, sir?'

'Well. Is it a person? A place? A deed of gift? What is it?'

'I can say, without any equivocation, that it is a person.'

'What person?'

'There you have me at a disadvantage.'

'Meaning?'

'It is impossible for me to name or otherwise identify this person.'

'Your reason?'

'I have sworn an oath to a certain individual.'

'The individual who gave you these papers?'

'The very same.'

Stevens looked at Ritson, who raised his eyebrows and feigned surprise.

Ireland cleared his throat, and looked once again out of the mullioned window.

'And you cannot give a name to this benefactor?'

'I can say no more. Do you wish me to violate a sacred pledge?'

'I beg your pardon?'

'I have sworn never to reveal my patron's name. Do you ask me to be dishonourable?'

'God forbid.'

Ireland glared at Stevens, as if he detected some irony in his response, but he was suddenly addressed by Ritson. 'Will this gentleman not come before us secretly, Mr Ireland?'

'I did not say he was a gentleman.'

'Not a gentleman?'

'Don't mistake my meaning. I am merely stating that I have not revealed the sex of my patron as yet.'

'Will this person, of whatever sex, come before us in the strictest confidence?'

'My patron has gone abroad. To Alsace.'

'For what reason?'

'My patron has been so disturbed in mind by this affair that London became insupportable.'

'It is all very unsatisfactory, Mr Ireland.'

'Nevertheless, Mr Stevens, it is the case.'

There was a rap upon the door. 'May I?' Samuel Ireland

entered the room and bowed to the committee. 'I am the father. This is not a court of law. By right I should be here.' He stood beside his son and smiled. 'William Ireland has no doubt removed the slightest shade of suspicion concerning my own actions in this affair.' He had heard everything William had said. 'Has he also informed you of his patron and benefactor?'

'Your son has referred to such an individual,' Stevens replied. 'But he has not yet gratified us with a name.'

'I have no name for you, sir. But I have confirmation of the gentleman's existence. I have seen him with my own eyes.' William looked at his father, and seemed to shake his head. 'He is of average height with a scar upon his left cheek which, he told me, was the result of an archery contest. He has a slight impediment in his speech, which I put down to shyness.'

'And where does this interesting gentleman live?'

'I believe he has lodgings in the Middle Temple. I cannot be certain –'

'Sir?'

'As my son has no doubt told you, he is a most elusive individual. He is presently abroad. I think he mentioned Alsace to me.'

Ritson then questioned Samuel Ireland about the nature and provenance of the Shakespearian documents, and in turn Ireland described to him his ever increasing astonishment and delight at the multitude of papers that his son carried into the bookshop. 'Here was God's plenty, gentlemen. It out-satisfied satisfaction.'

'That is very Shakespearian, sir.'

'It starved the eyes it fed, and the more it offered the more was wanted.'

'But can you tell us this, Mr Ireland, without ostentation.' Ritson had been looking keenly at William throughout this exchange, but now turned to Samuel. 'In your opinion, are these documents what they claim to be? Are they genuine Shakespearian productions?'

'That is not a question to put to a bookseller.'

'Forgive me. Was it indelicate?'

'I cannot claim to have any authority in such matters, sir.' He seemed to hesitate. 'Yet, on taking thought, I do believe these papers to be true and authentic. I flatter myself that I have an eye for detail. And I particularly noticed the thread holding together a bundle of manuscripts. It was very antique. A small token, perhaps, but —'

'But enough?'

'Enough to convince me that my son could not have invented such evidence.' He looked across at William. 'To have written. *Vortigern?* It is a thing impossible to conceive or to believe.'

As soon as they had walked out of Warwick Lane, William turned to him. 'Why did you lie about my patron?'

'Why did you? I doubt that she has gone to Alsace.'

'It is no matter where she has gone. She will not appear before them.' They walked a little way in silence. 'You should not have lied, Father. It is unlike you.'

'I wanted to assist you, William. You exonerated me, quite rightly, and I wished to express my support for you.'

'It can only lead to more lies. You should have stayed entirely away from this business.'

'Yet it concerns me.'

'Not to the extent of falsehood. You should reflect before

you speak, Father. You have plunged this whole affair into further uncertainty. A man with a scar on his face? With a stammer? Now I must contend with a wholly fictitious person. It is a complication. A hindrance.' He put his hands across his face. 'Do you not see how frightful it is?' He did not realise that he had sighed.

'I am sorry if I have alarmed you, William.'

'I feel as if I have no ground to stand upon. If you can lie on my behalf, then what do I have to support me?'

'Surely it is not so grave as that?'

'Do you believe the papers to be genuine, Father?'

'Of course I do. Why ask me that?'

'Then why mingle true with false? Why bring mud to the well? Do you not understand? Then it becomes a pit.'

Samuel Ireland was now growing angry with what he considered to be his son's impertinence; he told Rosa later that William had treated him as if he were a child. 'My mind has been much agitated, William. I have no rest either night or day but this business disturbs me.'

'I regret that very much. I have no wish to hurt you. I respect you.'

'Not enough. You wound me, William, with these criticisms. I cannot bear it.'

William cried out in the street. It was a howl, or a yell, that alarmed those hurrying past.

Samuel looked at his son in astonishment. 'Whatever is the matter?'

'And I did it all to please you!' With a desperate impatience William hailed down a chaise. 'Come with me, Father. This instant.' He did not speak on the short journey, but stared out of the window at the familiar streets and passages. As soon as they arrived in Holborn Passage he rushed into the bookshop and climbed the stairs to his room. He slammed the door shut, while his father waited for him in the shop below. Samuel was sweating slightly, and ran his hand along a shelf of early books that bore the word 'Incunabula'. For some reason he repeated aloud the refrain from an operetta, *The Musical Coalman*. 'Little house. Little house. Who lives in this little house?'

Then he heard the clattering of his son's boots on the wooden stairs. William came into the bookshop holding in his hand a sheet of old paper, brown and stained. 'Do you see this, Father? It is a true Shakespearian document.'

'But there is nothing written on it.'

'Precisely. Exactly.' William seemed to be fighting for breath. 'There is something I have been meaning to tell you.'

'Yes. The name. Give me the name of your patron.'

'There is no name. There is no patron.' William grabbed his father by the arm. 'I am the name.'

'I don't quite –' He studied his son's anxious, pleading features.

'Don't you see it? I am the benefactor. There was no lady in the coffee-house. I invented her.'

'What in God's name are you saying?' His throat had suddenly gone dry.

William then went down on his knees. 'I crave your pardon in the most submissive terms. I acted out of innocent delight and sheer intoxication with my gifts. I did it to please you –'

'Up, sir. Get up.' He struggled with his son, and slowly raised him to his feet.

'I have caused you much trouble, Father. I am sorry for it.'

'I know it. But all will be well if you give me the name of your benefactor.'

'You have not understood a word I have said. Listen to me, Father. There is no benefactor. I am responsible for the Shakespearian papers.'

'You mean that you found them?'

'I wrote them. I created them.'

'This is some pleasantry, William. Some riddle.'

'I assure you it is not. I fabricated all the documents you believe to be from the pen of Shakespeare.'

'I cannot listen to you.' He turned away and began examining the shelf of incunabula.

William took him by the shoulders and forced him to turn round. 'I can show you every detail of my forgery, from the ink to the seal. Do you wish to know how to create an ancient ink? I mixed the three different liquids used by book-binders in marbling the covers of their calf bindings. When they ferment they are imbued with a dark brown colour.'

'You are still protecting your patron. It is very noble.'

'I discoloured the papers with tobacco-water. Look at this sheet.' Samuel Ireland refused to notice it. 'Then I fumigated them with smoke. Why do you think I had a fire in the middle of summer?'

'No, no more. I refuse to believe you.'

'I obtained the paper from Mr Askew in Berners Street. He gave me fly-leaves from old folio and quarto volumes. He is so ancient that he had not the least suspicion of my intentions.'

'There is not a word of truth in any of this.'

'All is true, Father.'

'You can stand before me and tell me that you alone – no more than a boy – you alone produced such voluminous papers? It is laughable. It is ridiculous.'

'It is the truth.'

'No. Not truth. Phantasy. Your wits have been turned by this business. You can no longer distinguish between what is real and what is false. I know you, William.'

'You do not know me at all.'

'I know that there is no manner or method by which you could have counterfeited the style of Shakespeare.'

'I will do it now. This instant. I will show you, Father, how I am the forger. Come with me.'

'I will not come with you. These absurd falsehoods will convince nobody.'

'I will write you lines of Shakespeare that Mr Malone will deem wholly genuine.'

William turned, at a sudden noise. Someone had closed the door of the shop, and was hurrying away.

Mary Lamb had decided to deliver the letter to William Ireland in person. She had persuaded Charles to express his regret and surprise at the inquiry into the Shakespearian papers, and to confirm his faith in their authenticity.

'I hope it is not too much to expect from you,' she had said. 'I know how precious your time has become.' Yet he had delayed until, that Sunday morning, she had brought pen and ink to his room. He was still lying in his bed.

'It is time,' she said. 'I can wait no longer. I cannot leave William in torment.'

Charles observed her face, drawn and pale, and wondered if she were about to cry. 'Surely you are exaggerating, dear?'

'Not in the least. He is in peril. He is in danger.'

He did not wish to move her further, so he took the pen

and wrote a brief letter of support and encouragement. She snatched it from the pillow, on which Charles was leaning, and bore it in triumph out of the door. She returned to her own room, where she addressed an envelope to 'William Ireland, Esquire'. Then she took it up, and kissed the name. A few minutes later she hurried out of the house, and walked quickly to Holborn Passage. She was coming up to the door of the bookshop when she heard William telling his father that he had invented the woman in the coffee-house. She did not know what he meant, for a moment, and then she put her hand up to her mouth. She stopped, looked around slowly, and pushed the door further open.

William had lied to her. He had betrayed her. She found herself thinking of other things – of the flight of sparrows from dark corner to dark corner, of some broken glass upon the cobbles, of a linen curtain billowing in the breeze, of the leaden sky threatening rain. And then just as suddenly she felt very cheerful. Nothing could touch her. Nothing could hurt her. 'I am discharged from life,' she said to herself, 'after valiant service.'

She was moving quickly, not knowing or caring in which direction she was travelling, when she was filled with an over-powering sense of his absence. No one would ever walk beside her again. She had to sit down, to fight her rising feeling of panic, and sank upon a flight of steps leading to the church of St Giles-in-the-Fields.

The air was filled with the stench of horses when eventually she stood up and made her way home.

William Ireland turned back, having left the shop and seen Mary run down the passage. He had recognised her at once, but he had not called out to her.

He re-entered the shop. His father had turned around, and was walking slowly upstairs. William collected every item of Shakespearian material that he could find. He took the manuscript of *Vortigern* from a small cupboard below the stairs, and placed it with all the other papers and documents that he had once so carefully prepared and inscribed. He gathered up the unpublished pages of *Henry II* over which he had laboured in his room for many weeks and days, copying exactly the mode of writing which he had learned from Shakespeare's signatures. He went quietly upstairs to his own room and brought down the inks and sheets of paper that he had got ready for his work. Here also were scraps of manuscript, containing the jug watermark of Elizabeth's reign, which he had purchased from Mr Askew in Berners Street. He added books, the dedications of which he had lovingly fabricated, and small drawings which he had embellished. He took up a brimstone match, with a tinder-box, and lit the pile. It did not burn easily or quickly, but the ink and wax reacted with the flame to produce a billowing black smoke which filled the shop. William opened the door, but the sudden draught increased the fire. In the smoke he could not see the extent of the conflagration but he could hear it. The wooden floor and shelves were easily consumed, and then he noticed the flames leaping up the staircase.

Mary went straight to her room, and locked the door. Oh there is Tizzy calling me down for tea. What shall it be today?

India or China? I love the sound of the spoon in the cup. I love the tips of my fingers touching the rim of the cup. There was a knock upon the door. She put her face against it, sensing the coolness of the wood. 'I will be coming in a moment, Tizzy.'

'Don't let it get cold, Miss Lamb.'

'No. It will be hot.'

She waited until Tizzy had descended the stairs, and then she unlocked the door. She closed it quietly behind her, and listened intently for any sound below.

A few moments later Mary entered the kitchen, just as Mrs Lamb was adjusting her husband's napkin. 'Sit down, Mary, and begin. I wonder you have lived in this house for so long and can still mistake the time. Why? What is it?' Mary was staring at her mother, opening and closing her mouth as if she had been suddenly deprived of speech. 'Are you unwell?'

Mr Lamb started moaning – a low, constant moan – as Mary took up the teapot and held it in front of her as if she were defending herself. 'Can you not see what it is?' She was addressing her father.

'It is a teapot, Mary.' Mrs Lamb went towards her, and took her by the wrists. 'Put it down. This instant.'

There was a sudden struggle, and the teapot fell upon the table scattering the water and leaves all over the dark wood. Mary snatched up the fork, used for toasting crumpets over the fire, and plunged it deep into her mother's neck. Without a sound Mrs Lamb fell to the floor. At this moment Charles entered the kitchen, with a happy '*Buongiorno!*'

Chapter Fourteen

My dearest de Quincey,

   You will have been informed by now of the terrible calamities that have fallen on our family. My poor dear dearest sister in a fit of insanity has been the death of her own mother. She is at present in a mad-house from where I fear she will be moved to a prison and, God forbid, to the scaffold. God has preserved me to my senses — I eat and drink and sleep, and have my judgement I believe very sound. My father is further distracted, of course, and I am left to take care of him and our maid-servant. Thank God I am very calm and composed, and able to do the best that remains to do. Write — as religious a letter as possible — but no mention of what is gone and done with. With me 'the former things are passed away' and I have something more to do than to feel. I charge you, don't think of coming to see me. Write. I will not see

you if you come. God almighty love you and all of us –
C. Lamb

Once the first astonishment and dismay had passed, de
Quincey lay fully clothed upon the bed and looked at the
ceiling. Then he said aloud, 'What a fine story!'

A week later, a coroner and jury were convened in an upstairs
room of a public house in Holborn. Charles had arrived early,
and was sitting in the front row of seats. The chamber was
crowded with neighbours and spectators who had come to
witness the demeanour of what the *Westminster Gazette* had
called 'this unhappy young woman'. There had never before
been such a murder in Holborn.

Mary was brought into the jury's presence by the beadle of
the district, together with his deputy and the doctor of a private
mad-house in Hoxton where Mary was presently detained.
Her woeful expression, and the subdued manner in which she
followed the directions of the beadle and doctor, elicited
general sympathy. The sequence of events was read out to the
jury, and the doctor, Philip Girtin, was then questioned by the
coroner. He stated that he had examined the young woman
on three separate occasions and had concluded that she was
not in her right mind. He informed the jury that her derange-
ment had been provoked 'by a too sensitive mind', overwrought
'by the harassing fatigues of too many duties'. William Ireland
was not mentioned.

'Is she in any position to endure a trial?' the coroner asked
him.

'Most certainly not, sir. She is not in the least able to withstand such an ordeal. It would push her deeper into lunacy from which it would prove difficult to extract her.'

Throughout these proceedings Mary sat with her hands folded upon her lap. Occasionally she would look at Charles, but there was no expression upon her face.

'What would you propose then, Doctor Girtin?'

'I believe it best that this unfortunate female should be placed under my care in Hoxton. I do not believe that she is a danger to others, but I suggest that she be kept under restraint as long as I deem it to be necessary.'

'In case –'

'She may prove still to be a danger to herself.'

The jury agreed with the doctor's conclusions. Mary was released into the custody of Philip Girtin, and in a ritual of the coroner's court her arms were bound to her sides with a leather strap.

When Charles left the public house, he feared that he would never see his sister again beyond the confines of the madhouse. As he walked back to Laystall Street he realised that he had been crying.

Charles's fears proved to be unfounded. In the care of Philip Girtin, Mary began to recover her senses. The doctor read to her from Gibbon and from Tyndale, and at those times it seemed to her that she was conversing again with her brother; he engaged her in games of cribbage and primero, to test her grasp of numeracy as well as literacy. She began to discuss with him the poems of Homer, and took great delight in quoting from Shakespeare.

He had forbad Charles her presence, fearing that the associations would prove too painful, but after three months of her confinement he asked her brother to visit Hoxton. His study overlooked a garden where Mary and the other patients were sitting. 'I have just returned from the Home Office,' he told him. 'I have seen the Commissioner of Lunacy on the subject of your sister. He agrees with me that she will be secure in your company as long as you give your solemn engagement that you will take her under your care for life.'

'Of course. That is the least –'

'I require you to visit her here each evening for a period of a fortnight. I must know whether you excite her too much.'

'I will remind her?'

'Precisely. But if that test is passed, as I believe it will be, then we will proceed to her eventual release. All must be calm and orderly, Mr Lamb.'

Charles looked out of the window at her. She was sewing, occasionally looking up at the other patients.

Charles moved to a new house in Islington, beside the New River, and here Mary renewed her life of freedom. When he went to his employment in East India House, she was cared for by Tizzy's niece; Tizzy had retired to a small property in Devizes, but had declared that she could not leave Charles and Mary in the hands of a 'stranger'. Mr Lamb had died from advanced senility a few months after his wife's murder. His last words, muttered to Charles, had been, 'And that's true, too.'

In new surroundings Mary remained for the most part calm and even serene. As Charles wrote to de Quincey soon after her arrival in Islington,

My poor dear dearest sister is restored to her senses; to a dreadful sense and recollection of what has passed, awful to her mind, but tempered with a religious resignation and the reasonings of a sound judgement which knows how to distinguish between a deed committed in a transient fit of frenzy and the terrible guilt of a mother's murder.

In the evenings, after Charles's return from Leadenhall Street, they sat together and conversed on every subject. Then by degrees they began to collaborate on writing stories taken from the plays of Shakespeare. They found it impossible to agree upon who had initiated the idea, each one trying to assign that honour to the other, but it proved remarkably successful. The first volume, published by Liveright & Elder, received much critical praise in *Westminster Words*, the *Gentleman's Magazine* and the other periodicals.

There were occasions, however, when Mary was not so composed. She had said to Charles, for example, 'Thoughts come unbidden to me. Do you see them flying about the room?' Her distress grew more palpable and ominous. At these times Charles would accompany her over the fields to the private mad-house in Hoxton; she would take her strait-jacket with her, and willingly surrender herself to Philip Girtin. De Quincey had written to Charles, after hearing of one such episode:

I look upon you as a man called by sorrow and anguish and

by a strange desolation of hopes, into quietness, and a soul set apart, and made peculiar to God.

The fire started in the bookshop by William Ireland, on that fateful Sunday, had claimed no victims.

'I smell sausages,' Rosa Ponting had said.

'No, my love. That is smoke.' Samuel Ireland had walked to the top of the staircase, and had seen the flames in the bookshop.

'Oh my lord,' was all he said.

He rushed over and grabbed Rosa just as she was about to take up a roasted egg from the fender. 'Wherever are we going, Sammy? What is it?'

'Out. Up.'

He pushed her out of the room, and hauled her up the two flights of stairs to their bedroom. The window here looked over a neighbour's balcony in Holborn Passage. 'I cannot squeeze through that, Sammy. I really cannot do it.'

'Very well. Do you want to be boiled like suet?'

He thrust open the window, breaking its sash in the process, and somehow she managed to press herself through the available space.

Shortly after they escaped, the whole house was consumed in flame.

The Shakespearian papers were destroyed. That had been William's intention. Soon after the fire he had written a letter to his father – who, with Rosa, had moved to Winchelsea – in which he asked for forgiveness.

That I have been guilty of a fault in giving you the manuscripts, I confess and am sorry for it. But I must at the same
time assure you that it was done without a bad intention, or
even a thought of what would ensue. As you have repeatedly
stated to me that 'truth will find its basis' even so will your
character, notwithstanding any malignant aspersion, soon
appear unblemished in the eyes of the world.

Samuel Ireland never replied to his son.

William then published a sixpenny pamphlet entitled *The
Recent Fabrications of Shakespeare Exposed and Explained by Mr W.
H. Ireland Who is Himself the Sole Agent and Actor of These False
Transactions*. He concluded his account with a 'general apology'
in which he stated that 'I did not intend injury to anyone. I
really injured no one. I did not produce the papers from any
pecuniary motive. I by no means benefited by the papers', and
added that 'Being scarcely seventeen years and a half old my
boyhood should have in some measure screened me from the
malice of my persecutors'. A paragraph in the *Morning Chronicle*
aptly summarised the public response to this production.
'W. H. Ireland has come forward and announced himself
author of the papers attributed by him to Shakespeare; which,
if *true*, proves him to be a *liar*.'

In the summer of 1804 Mary Lamb suffered one of her more
prolonged attacks. She had been confined in the mad-house
for several weeks when Philip Girtin spoke to Charles, who
had been visiting his sister.

'She needs occupation,' he said. 'Entertainment.'

'What do you suggest, Doctor Girtin?'

'She has told me that she once directed a play with you and your friends. Is that correct?'

'Certainly. We were rehearsing some scenes from *A Midsummer Night's Dream*, when – when she became ill.'

'Can you not revive them? It may offer her some sense of life as, how can I put it, continuous.'

So Charles had persuaded Tom Coates and Benjamin Milton to present with him a slimmer version of the play of the mechanicals. They had been wary of entering a private madhouse, but Charles had emphasised to them the cleanliness, brightness and good order of Philip Girtin's establishment. 'Besides,' he said, 'I am sure that it will greatly assist Mary in her recovery.'

So they agreed to take on the roles of Pyramus and Thisbe, while Charles would 'double' as Bottom and the Wall. On one Sunday afternoon, in late spring, they donned their costumes in an adjacent parlour and then appeared before a group of Girtin's patients who were sitting on small chairs in the communal dining-chamber, some fifteen of them, including Mary Lamb. The males were all dressed in black coats, white waistcoats, black silk breeches and stockings. Their hair was powdered and frizzed, to accentuate the extraordinary neatness of their appearance. The ladies were dressed in no less elegant style with embroidered cotton gowns, green shawls and mob-caps.

Charles had decided to vary the theatrical entertainment with some passages from the speeches of Theseus and Oberon in the same play; but he would leave out the lines of Theseus concerning

> *The lunatic, the lover, and the poet*
> *Are of imagination all compact.*

All appeared to be going well, except that the audience had the habit of sitting solemnly through the comic scenes and laughing heartily at the more serious perorations. Mary Lamb, sitting in the front row, seemed to delight in all the impersonations. She particularly enjoyed the performance of Benjamin Milton as Thisbe, and laughed out loud when he chanted his lament over the body of Pyramus:

> *'This cherry nose,*
> *These yellow cowslip cheeks,*
> *Are gone, are gone!*
> *Lovers, make moan;*
> *His eyes were green as leeks!'*

She only grew restless when her brother stepped forward in the role of Oberon and began to recite the final speech:

> *'To the best bride-bed will we,*
> *Which by us shall blessed be;*
> *And the issue there create*
> *Ever shall be fortunate.'*

She sighed very loudly when he spoke the line, '*Ever true in loving be*', and then suddenly leaned forward as if intending to pray. But her arms were dangling by her sides. As Tom Coates said later, 'she died as quietly as she had lived'. The cause of her death was later pronounced to be 'disorder of the arteries'.

William Ireland did not abandon the world of writing. He published more than sixty-seven books, among them *Ballads in*

Imitation of the Antients and *Neglected Genius. A Poem Illustrating the Untimely and Unfortunate Fate of Many British Poets. Containing Imitations of Their Different Styles.*

He also opened a subscription library in Kennington. Among the books that he sent out to borrowers was *Tales from Shakespeare* by Charles and Mary Lamb. He never again alluded to his own Shakespearian adventure. But every year, on the anniversary of Mary Lamb's death, he left a bouquet of red flowers beside her grave at St Andrew's, Holborn. Charles Lamb grew old in the service of the East India Company, together with Tom Coates and Benjamin Milton, and was buried in the same churchyard.

BY PETER ACKROYD
ALSO AVAILABLE IN VINTAGE

☐ Albion	0099438070	£16.99
☐ Blake	0749391766	£9.99
☐ Brief Lives: Chaucer	009928748X	£7.99
☐ The Clerkenwell Tales	0749386304	£6.99
☐ Dan Leno and the Limehouse Golem	0749396598	£6.99
☐ Dickens	0749306475	£12.50
☐ Dickens (Abridged)	0099437090	£7.99
☐ The Life of Thomas More	0749386401	£8.99
☐ London: The Biography	0099422581	£12.99
☐ Milton in America	0749386258	£6.99
☐ The Collection	0099428946	£12.99
☐ The Plato Papers	0099289954	£6.99